Reagan Hawk

A King's Ransom

RAVEN

The Raven Books

A King's Ransom (Masters of Pleasure)
Cover art © copyright 2013, Eliza Black

A King's Ransom © copyright 2013, Reagan Hawk
First Print Edition Publication May 2013, The Raven Books
First Electronic Printing May 2013, The Raven Books
Edited by Suz Gower
Final Line Edited by Dianne B
ALL RIGHTS RESERVED.

ISBN-13: 978-1-62501-046-9
ISBN-10: 162501046X

WWW.THERAVENBOOKS.COM

www.RavenHappyHour.com

A King's Ransom

Reagan Hawk

Reagan Hawk Books

Strength in Numbers Series
Strength in Numbers
Space Pirates' Bounty
Bounty Hunters' Captive

The Beast Masters Series
Trading Teon
Securing Sara
Rescuing Reya
Capturing Clara
Binding Bree

Masters of Pleasure Series
A King's Ransom
A Knight's Redemption
A Prince's Captive

Cyber Sex Series
Prepared to Please
Denial of Service
Programmed for Pleasure

Dedication

To Michelle Pillow, for answering the phone no matter the day or night, for not laughing when I threaten to go on a brownie-eating binge if my characters don't start to obey my every wish, but mostly for helping to hold my hand and kick me square in the butt when called for during the writing of this book. To Shane, you read through each chapter faithfully, made the brownies I was craving and told me time and time again that I could do this. To my editors, thank you for all you do! And to my readers, what a wild ride we've been on together. Thank you! Now, I'd like some more brownies.

Chapter One

City of Vesta in the Kingdom of Tamonius on the Planet Panucia...

Kritan of Katarius walked through the streets of Vesta, a city known across the planet for its corruption and wickedness. He drew his black cloak around him more—to hide the sword at his side and the dagger in the top of his left boot. The clothing he wore was appropriate for the area, though nothing he'd normally want upon his body—the material was something a commoner would wear and not to his liking. He preferred trews to the tunic with a roped belt. He liked his boots, not the ones he wore now that were more of a sandal, leaving some of his foot exposed. He disliked, too, the ring that held his sword, preferring his sheath. He had not dared to bring his personal sword and shield. They were things that would give his origins—and his role—away.

It was important to blend. At least for now.

Cool wind from the north, from across the Ice Seas, blew past him. It was welcome against the heat of Tamonius's summer. Kritan preferred slightly cooler weather. While he could warm his body naturally by allowing his beast to rise, he could not cool it as easily.

His lip curled at the sight of three women standing, their breasts hanging out of the tops of their tunics. They were whores. His homeland, Katarius, was not without pleasures of the flesh, but they did not openly display their sexuality as the people of Tamonius did. While Katarius had whores, the guards there policed the streets better, making sure the women who charged were corralled into taverns or brothels, not left to wander the streets aimlessly for any and all to see. So far Kritan had lost count of the number of women he'd seen since entering the walls of Vesta who were selling their bodies for a few measly coins or even stale bread.

Such a state of things. And the Tamoni thought they were so superior to the six occupied countries on their home planet.

Kritan walked with his head up, moving with purpose, though he was not yet sure of where he needed to be. His informant had spoken of a tavern four roads within the gates of Vesta. As Kritan walked the length of the fourth row, he could count at least five taverns directly around him, each filthier than the last.

Unease settled over him. He had known this would be a fool's mission. One he should not have undertaken himself, but he'd had no choice. He had to find his brother. He had to make amends, and he would walk through the cesspool called Vesta a thousand times over if he thought it would give him a chance to make things right. Banishing Jaelyn all those years ago had been a mistake. One he'd lived with for nearly two decades. Lies and a woman—a woman Kritan had believed meant more to him than she did—had fostered an environment that left him speaking words he could not take back, and sending his brother far from home. So long had gone by with no word on his brother's whereabouts, that when a missive arrived telling a tall tale—one that spoke of Jaelyn not only being alive but in grave danger, so much so that his brother was suddenly on borrowed time, Kritan could not stop himself. He'd mounted a steed and set forth on a quest to find the man—to hell with the cost. Regardless that he had men to do such things for him. That, as King of Katarius, rushing alone into the kingdom of Tamonius was not simply reckless, it was suicide. This was his brother and he would right the wrong he'd committed long ago.

"You look like you like it rough," a whore said, cupping her unimpressive breasts as she wiggled for him. It was clear to see the woman had serviced many cocks in her days and life had not been kind to her.

Her friend and fellow whore slinked her arms over the woman's shoulders and flicked her tongue, as if being offered a threesome would create a more appealing sight for him to behold. Kritan was no stranger to threesomes, foursomes and more. But he would never soil himself with the likes of these women. All the face paint in the kingdom could not hide the signs of disease on their skin, and the reek of strong spirits they'd been drinking could not mask the fact they had not bathed in months. Maybe more. Both looked heavily used and past their prime. Neither motivated his cock.

He had been too long between fucks and should have felt his beast stirring, wanting release. As a Katarian male shifter he was immune to the diseases that plagued the non-shifters—sexual or not. Though dirty whores never tempted him. He had certain standards, ones belonging to a king. There were many women who begged to be at his service within his castle, ready to ease his cock should he but click his fingers. All were screened by him before being granted such a coveted position. And sometimes, when he felt randy, he would sneak away to the buttery with a serving wench or two.

Regardless how long it had been since he'd fucked, his focus remained firm—find his brother.

Find Jaelyn.

Nothing else mattered.

"Perhaps he doesn't like cunt," stated the taller whore with an ungodly cackle.

Her friend grabbed a third female, this one smaller, and thrust her at him. "You like your cunt young? You can take her and pretend she's your—"

Grunting, Kritan held up a hand, stopping the crass woman from going on. The girl could not have seen more than seventeen summers. Reaching under his cloak, he found his coin purse and withdrew a gold coin. He flicked it to the oldest of the women and leveled his hard gaze upon her. The beast pulsed in him, wanting free, wanting to silence the older woman.

The young girl was but a child in his eyes and that of the beast, and both believed children should be cherished and protected, not sold to whomever could pay. He knew his dark eyes now danced with icy-blue flecks and he knew what a show of power such a thing presented to the lowborns. "Take this child from the streets. Feed her. See she sleeps in a proper bed without a man sharing it, and if I see her upon these streets again, or hear of your whoring her out again, I will take your head from your neck. Am I clear?"

The woman clutched the gold coin and nodded, backing away from him. "The devil is in his eyes," she whispered.

Her accomplice gasped. "His eyes reflect the light. Like an animal!"

The young girl was the only one who didn't look scared of him. He supposed he was one of only a few men to turn down the offer of time with her, and he guessed she held no desire to be part of the life that had damaged her acquaintances. She didn't move as she stared up at him with a faint smile touching her lips. "Thank you, sir."

With a nod, he left them as they hurried away. He knew he'd put enough fear into the older two that for at least a few nights they'd keep the younger woman off the streets. Such was the way of things in Vesta. If it were under his rule, so much would change.

So much depravity would never have been permitted.

He was not a cruel leader. He did not rule through fear, but he did rule all the same. He was respected, and while he understood there were certain elements of society that would never change, he did what he could to control it by whatever means necessary.

Vesta had strayed from the path centuries before Kritan's birth. Stories told of it once being a great city full of knowledge, arts and technologies. That was long ago. A time nearly forgotten. He did not know what had prompted its downfall, but it was evident it had indeed fallen. He wasn't sure it could be saved or if the inhabitants even wanted the help.

A street peddler approached, his cart of wares jingling as he walked. The end of the street looked as though it might still be used as a market. Though, to sell what, Kritan wasn't sure. No reputable person of Tamonius would be caught dead in this section of the city—that is, if reputable persons even existed anymore in the kingdom. He was fast beginning to doubt any did.

The cloaked man, pushing the vendor cart, smelled of mortality and sickness. Dirt clung to his cloak, coating the lower portion the most, as if he'd walked through his fair share of slop. The man slowed his pace as he neared Kritan. "What have you?" the man asked. "Got me a bit of anythin' you might be wantin', sir."

Kritan tried to ignore him, but the man lifted his arms, causing Kritan's hand to go to the hilt of his sword. The man stared out from one good eye, the other a mass of scars and what looked to be old burns. "None of that now, boy."

Boy?

Kritan held his tongue. He was far older than this man. He was older than most.

"I've the finest goods you'll find this part of Vesta," the vendor said, motioning to his street cart. "If you're into the finer things, which I can tell you are, I've decommissioned pieces. The kind others can't come by. It's my specialty."

Alarm raced through Kritan. Most technologies had been banned centuries ago. To be caught with pieces that weren't fully decommissioned could mean prison. He did not need to be detained now because some street vendor wanted to turn a profit.

11

Upon closer look, he could see glimpses of old objects once used during the Age of Space Travel. An age that had left the people of Panucia with too much power and too little self-restraint. It was before Kritan's time, but he'd heard enough stories from his father to know it was a time best left alone.

"Be gone, old man," Kritan said sternly. "I want nothing to do with what you sell."

He did not need guards poking around, and the vendor was sure to bring them about. The old man shrugged and turned, pushing his cart and mumbling as he went. "Youngin' think they know the way of things. They know nothing."

Light shone from the tavern nearest Kritan. He pushed the thin, worn material to the side in the entranceway and entered. A serving wench nearly plowed into him, her hands full with a tray of mead. She scoffed at him and then carried on with her duties, placing full mugs of ale before already-drunken patrons.

Someone played a flute to the right and the sound was nearly drowned out by the volume of the locals. Kritan's nostrils flared as the smell of sex washed over him. Sweat. Dirt. Cunt. Cum. Piss and shit.

He stiffened, fighting the urge to lose his lunch.

Filthy heathens.

His gaze moved to the barkeep and then around the room. He looked for a man with a gold wolf brooch. That was what his informant would be wearing. Something the Tamoni wouldn't normally be caught in. They disliked the beasts from the Northeast greatly. The feeling was mutual. The Katarian held no love for the Tamoni. Kritan knew there was no love lost between Tamonius and the other occupied countries on Panucia. The Vamone's hatred of the Tamoni made the Katarian's thoughts on them look downright loving.

No fault could be placed on the Vamone. Tamonius continued to launch raids against them, stealing their women and taking slave labor.

Kritan would not be here if it was not for his brother. The thought kept him centered and focused.

Several of the men looked towards him. Some wore the colors of the Tamoni army—mercenaries who once had order and training behind them but who now worked for senators as guards and hired thugs. Others looked to be civilians out for a good time. As a full-figured woman lifted her tunic high, exposing her sex, two men shoved her back onto a tabletop.

"That's right, men, step up if you think you've got what it takes to impress me," she said, her accent heavy. She lacked front teeth and had at least a week's worth of grime upon her face and arms. The men did not seem to care. "I will be the judge of whose cock is bigger. Stick them in me. I'll test them just right."

Men lined up and Kritan held his tongue, glancing around, looking for a man with a gold brooch as the woman permitted man after man to take his turn with her. She lay there laughing, sticking her tongue out and pushing several men away by their foreheads so that another could join in the fun. The entire ordeal was revolting. Kritan would never understand the ways or thoughts of the Tamoni.

He exited the establishment, pleased to be free of the scents within. Being one with a beast, and being able to smell things others outside of his kind could not, often left him sensitive to odors. Sounds and light as well. Vesta was full of everything but light. He had yet to see it during the daytime, but he half wondered if the sun's rays could not penetrate through the horrors of Vesta.

His soft boots crunched the gravel mix beneath his feet. He made his way to the next tavern. He slowed his pace as two men stumbled from the entrance.

"You should see the fine piece of cunt I just fucked," one said, swaying to the left and then so far to the right Kritan assumed he'd fall over. Somehow he managed to stay upright.

His companion smiled wide, showing off rotted teeth. "Like virgin cunt. Tight. Tender body."

The other nodded. "She was the best I've ever seen. Nothing like chained cunts to satisfy a man and his needs. Three of 'em in there. Sisters. Fine fucks. You can stick your prick in them anywhere you want, as much as you want so long as you buy yourself a drink first."

Chained women?

"Looked like three virgins of loveliness," said the swaying man.

"But the way their pussies milked my cock says they've known much dick," the other added. "Just as a woman should."

Kritan's temper rose, at odds with his need to find Jaelyn and his need to smash in the faces of these lowborns. He couldn't in good conscience allow three women to be chained sex slaves.

One of the men clasped his hand on Kritan's shoulder. "Try their asses too."

Kritan shrugged the man off and entered the tavern. He was struck instantly with the scent of rotting flesh—corpses. He stilled, wondering why they would keep the long dead among the living. Vesta continued to surprise him when he thought himself a worldly man.

The patrons were rowdy, all gathered around, forming a circle with an open center. Kritan spotted chains hooked to the ceiling. As the crowd parted slightly, he expected to see the three bound young women. What he saw shocked his senses. He was wrong. The smell wasn't from corpses. Three old hags were naked and bound, each grinning wider than the next as they performed various sex acts upon the patrons.

They were old—very old—from before the height of Panucia's Age of Space Travel. They smelled of death and magik. As Kritan

14

caught sight of one of their inner arms, he spotted the witch's mark. He knew then what they were. Fornication Hags. It made sense. They were thought to be extinct, having last been seen in the Valley of the Dead some eight centuries ago. Kritan had thought the rumors of their abilities to wield glamour to be greatly exaggerated. How could these men not see what was before them? How could they not see that what they were so eager to stick their pricks into was a hag as old as time? It was clear by the drunken taunts from the crowd that the lowborn, non-magiks clamoring for a chance to stick their cocks in the cackling hags did not see what was truly there. The fables of the Fornication Hags had not done them justice.

It was said those without magik or with limited magik would look upon them and see them as virginal young women, flawless and highly sexual. In reality, they were ancient and fed off sex and lust. Each man who dared to thrust their cock inside them ran the risk of becoming part of their thrall—to be called upon by them at a later date, forced to serve their every whim. At this rate the three would have the whole of the Vesta tavern district enthralled by the end of the month.

One of the hags was on her hands and knees before a man who wore a high-end tunic—a sign the highborns without magik were not immune to the hags' charms either. The man's cock was deep in her mouth and he looked swept up in the act.

The men around the one getting his cock sucked cheered and lifted their mugs of mead into the air. "Finish with her, I want a turn."

"Fi-ll her belly w-with your seed," another said, his speech slightly slurred as if he'd had too much drink.

The ignorant fools had no idea what was truly before them. What they were giving away for a chance at perceived bliss.

Their souls.

The hag nearest Kritan paused, her gaze moving to him. A sickening smile danced upon her face. She winked and then brought her index finger to her lips. "Shhh."

A nod was all he offered. He held no love for the locals and it was evident they were not worth his pity or intervention. The hags could keep their secret. What did he care if they took over the entire city? Would anyone notice? Could it be any worse than it was? He had a mission and they were not part of it. Besides, they had to be doing something with the power they collected from the sexual encounters. He didn't want to become the target for it.

Movement from the corner of the tavern caught Kritan's attention. A man with a brown cloak stood there. A gold wolf pin was fastened to the cloak. A sense of relief washed over Kritan. He would not be forced to endure any more taverns on his hunt for his informant. He had found him. His contact motioned for Kritan to follow him as he pushed back a worn, red cloth that hung in a darkened doorway.

All of Kritan's senses lit, on the ready in case it was a trap. He walked past the three hags. One touched his leg. "Sire, let us please you. It has been so long since we serviced one of your kind."

He resisted the urge to jerk back from her touch, instead schooling his face. He didn't need them sending their thralls after him because he'd injured their pride. "I am on a quest. Perhaps after."

More like never. No amount of ale or spirits would make them appear as anything more than they were and he did not want to have to chew off his own arm to escape them come morning.

More like I'd have to burn off my own cock should it happen into one of them.

She released him, content with his response.

Stepping past the material, Kritan took a deep breath. Sex. The scent was everywhere. He couldn't escape it. Small oil lamps hung from the corridor's ceiling, providing very little in the way of light. As a Katarian, he required little to be able to see. He suspected the lighting was as such so those passing within the hall would not easily recognize one another. If he was right, this tavern was much more than a place to drink and eat. It was a Den of Debauchery—where one could come to get their every sexual desire fulfilled, no matter how perverse. And it was more than likely run by someone with great magik. It would explain the Fornication Hags and the overwhelming sense of desire that seemed to float through the air.

There was a flicker from the far right and then the scent of something he could not believe would be happening so brazenly and in the open. Sex acts were one thing, but to use forbidden technologies was another. Kritan watched in stunned surprise as a holographic image of a woman sputtered in and out of focus. She was nude and squeezing her ample breasts while she darted her tongue in and out over her lower lip.

The entire ordeal might have looked erotic and enticing had the technology been in proper working order.

"Drink up," she said, the sound quality dismal, probably from the age of the technology and neglect. The patrons raised their mugs and shouted for refills, all while continuing to fuck or watch others fuck the Fornication Hags.

What a hole in the ground.

Vesta was notorious for Dens of Debauchery. As was the whole of Tamonius. His kingdom was not without its establishments of ill repute, but it did not flaunt them the way Tamonius did. Higher-end dens in his kingdom were regulated and taxed. The business was profitable and in the end the regulations meant the women were clean and disease-free and well treated by the den owners and operators.

The scent of fresh blood came over Kritan, drawing him from his thoughts of home. He paused, the wolf within wanting to know more. Blood excited the animal. Always had and always would. Kritan pushed

17

one of the curtains aside and spotted a peasant girl astride a man, a knife in her hand as she pulled it down his chest deep enough to draw blood, but not enough to cause real injury. The man's eyes were closed as he thrust up into her cunt. He enjoyed the pain, the blood.

Kritan could not walk away from the sight of the act. On some level he enjoyed the show. The beast in him longed for the freedom to draw blood during sex. The man in him, while repulsed at the idea of causing his lover that type of pain, was curious as well. He was so caught up in the scene before him that he didn't sense the men gathering around him until it was far too late. He knew then the blood sex act had been staged. It had been there to confuse his senses. To mask what he now smelled clearly.

Guards.

And they had come in numbers he could not win against.

Chapter Two

Three weeks later, outside the city of Vesta in the House of Argyros…

Surina walked along the outskirts of her father's country estate, clutching one of her favorite enchanted scrolls to her chest. The afternoon was peaceful and the weather cool enough for her to be able to enjoy walking about freely.

The estate was impressive, but she often felt as if it were a cage rather than a model of elegance, class and social standing. The gardens were the envy of all who visited and often wove in and out of one another, creating a maze she enjoyed getting lost within. When she was young she'd spent hours upon hours playing on the estate.

Surina would much rather be in the city where her father kept a home. Unfortunately, her father did not care much for city life. Buildings stacked side by side, crowded streets, brothels abounded and beggars on every corner. It was too much chaos for his tastes and far too much, in his opinion, for his innocent daughter. He often spoke of the depravity and thievery that was rampant within the city walls, though Surina was sure he tended to exaggerate when the need suited him.

His lectures on pickpockets, vagabonds, Dens of Debauchery and every other vile thing he could think to frighten her with often fell on deaf ears and were rivaled only by Surina's head guard's lectures on dangers. If her father was not preaching to her about the dangers of the world, Rawlin was. Both took great pride and pleasure in attempting to scare her to the point she should be afraid to leave the grounds without an army at her back. She had been beyond the city home's thick walls on several occasions and never ran into trouble.

How bad could Vesta really be? She was educated, not some small-minded thinker. A little bit of naughty behavior would not shock her.

19

And she was sure Vesta could not be as bad as her father described. It could not be the cesspool he made it out to be.

When Rawlin had learned that she had managed to sneak off unguarded, he'd threatened to make her wear a bell and to tie her to his side with magik. He was powerful enough to do such a thing. For the first time she was thankful her father and Rawlin could not fit her with a device to track her every move. Had such things not been rendered illegal, they just might have. All too quickly they would have had her fitted with something to alert them to her mischief.

Surina enjoyed venturing to the city on those rare occasions she was gifted the opportunity, though each time was during daylight hours and only for a very short duration. Her favorite way to pass the time was to visit the scroll vendors and the bakery. There was nothing better than an interesting read and a sweet treat. When able to sneak away while on a visit to the city, she often returned to the country home with stacks upon stacks of reading material and goodies to eat.

Her father, due to return to the country estate soon, would frown upon her wandering the property without a guard near her at all times. He'd talk of the state of things—the tensions between Tamonius and Katarius. In the past, the rival kingdoms had never shared more than a loose peace. As a prominent senator and a successful businessman who made a living in the trade industry, he had strong reasons to believe war was imminent.

She loved her father dearly, but he was overprotective and his endless lectures were tedious. To hear him talk of it, he believed when war finally came, the enemy would beat down the doors and take his only child from him—it mattered not that she was a young woman, already well into what was considered suitable marrying age. It had been nearly five full summers since she turned eighteen and was shown off to society. No, she would forever be his child. His baby girl.

And no man would ever be good enough for her.

20

At least according to her father.

Surina wondered to what extent her father made more of the situation between Tamonius and Katarius than was warranted. Maybe there wasn't really a threat of war, but just unrest. It was hard to tell with him since he was pre-disposed to making a tale taller than need be. He had once told of the giants that roamed the Valley of the Dead—a place where the unwanted went to dwell. Where the undesirables from each kingdom were banished and where there was no law, no order. Only death, pain and evil.

She had been six summers at the time and still remembered the way her father had embellished his tale of the giants—each time telling it he made them more fearsome, more horrible, more eager to gobble her up if she dared misbehave. She had been afraid to sleep without a candle lit for weeks.

When her father was near, Surina had to be on her best behavior even now, into her twenties. She was to be a lady at all times. To conduct herself in a way becoming to a prominent senator's daughter. But when her father was away, such as now, she could easily slip past her guard detail for some privacy. Rawlin was not so easy to fool, but often he was pulled away for one thing or another, leaving her with the others. It took little in the way of skill to outwit them. And it was not as if they were going to report losing her to Rawlin or her father.

Surina disliked having a guard shadow her every move in the one place she should feel totally safe—home. It had been that way for close to six full turns of the moon. She was a young woman with needs. It was nearly impossible to masturbate with servant girls always hovering about her in her chambers and guards always shadowing her every move. No one would permit her to be courted and no guard would dare touch her—not that she would let them.

Well, perhaps one. But Rawlin would not go against her father. Though Rawlin was the clear choice for her. He was handsome, brave, kind-hearted, yet fierce when need be.

She paused. The only problem was, Rawlin did not cause her chest to tighten when thinking of him. He did not stir unadulterated desire in her as she had read true loves should. Though, she did love him. It was all so confusing. Was the true love she'd read of a myth? Could it be the stories telling of undeniable attraction and desire where just that—stories?

She sighed. It was such a beautiful cage she lived in, but a cage all the same.

The *haynaiums* were in bloom. They only did so once a year, when the cool winds of the north blew through the valleys and countryside. Their vines were thick with thorns, but their flowers so delicate they would wilt should a strong breeze blow upon them. She ran her finger over one of the blossoms and, sure enough, it closed almost instantly, retreating into the shelter of its protective casing and steely wall of thorns. One day she'd hold one of their blooms in her hand and be able to touch its beauty as well as see it. Today, however, was not that day.

She took a seat on one of the benches and gave a quick look around to make sure she was still alone. Hesitantly, she unrolled the erotic scroll. The risk of being caught with something so scandalous added to the excitement, making her pulse speed. She liked feeling wild and wanton. She didn't want to be perfect and a model of grace.

Quickly lost in the tale it told, she squirmed in her seat, her breath quickening. The tale was one of lust and forbidden love. It spoke in detail of the hero doing explicit things to the heroine before he was drawn off to war, never to return. The scroll was frowned upon in many high-society homes, seen as nothing more than smut—a tale to wet the thighs of women and put foolish notions in their heads about marriage, and being about love and lust, rather than duty and bloodlines. Such tales were something only lowborns would busy themselves with. Certainly not something a lady would be caught with in her possession, and yet Surina read it as often as she could. It was a guilty pleasure.

She did not wish to marry for anything other than love, though she strongly suspected her father would not permit her to marry at all, regardless the reasons.

In her circles, erotic scrolls were hard to come by. She'd gotten this one by way of a friend of the family. The woman, having seen forty summers by then, had winked and left the scroll upon Surina's bed, telling her all young women should know passion as what was penned upon the parchment. Surina longed for a love affair like the one she read of. Longed to love a man so much she'd give herself to him freely, completely and forever.

She read the scroll again, focusing on the part that spoke of the man trailing kisses over the woman, straight down to the woman's cunt. Surina could hardly believe such a thing occurred.

Her personal maids, said to have originated from offworld and, at the very least, other kingdoms, often whispered of the pleasures to be had from a man's tongue upon a woman's clit. Surina tingled with desire and her pussy dampened at the thought of a man's mouth there. She wanted such an experience. Her maids and attendants had offered more than once to show her—to do those things to her. She didn't dislike the idea of a woman's face between her thighs but it did not hold the same appeal that the idea of a man doing so did. Besides, should she permit her maids to pleasure her and they be caught, they would be punished severely, possibly sold, which could mean their deaths, should they end up in a household that was not kind.

No. She would see to her own needs.

Surina inched her hand under her tunic and then moved it to her inner thigh. She bit at her lower lip as she eased her hand towards her pussy. Drawing upon her magik, she tapped into the scroll's enchantments. Within seconds the ink came to life, forming tiny figures, acting out the scenes written within. Magiks were permitted, where technologies were not, a loophole she greatly enjoyed exploiting.

The figures merged, coupling in a carnal way that excited her. She rubbed her clit more, working herself into a frenzy. Pleasure danced around the edges of her vision. So close. She was so close to release. She rubbed faster as one figure pounded into the other in the most beastly, feral way that she couldn't help but long for such a claiming. She wanted a man to take her in such a way. To make her burst with desire.

She tensed, biting her lip to keep from crying out and alerting her guards to her location, her legs shaking slightly as pleasure washed over her. With an unsteady breath, she withdrew her hand from under her tunic and tapped the scroll, returning the figures to nothing more than ink upon parchment. Shouts caught her attention, pulling her from her erotic daydreaming and lazy afternoon of self-pleasuring.

She stood quickly, fearful she'd be caught in a compromising position and with a forbidden scroll. Surina tucked the scroll into the waistband of her tunic, adjusting her *palla* over it to hide it from view. She followed the sound of the voices. When she neared the rows of endless *haynaiums*, the voices grew even louder. Familiar ones and some not so familiar. She stilled, her hand going to the scroll, her fingers brushing over the parchment as she considered turning back. Should her father discover she read those things, he would forbid her the few freedoms she had left.

The voices grew louder. One voice in particular belonged to a man who fancied himself in charge in her father's absence. In actuality, Dasin was fairly low down on the chain of command. While he did have a small group of guards assigned to him, he wasn't what anyone, other than himself, would consider to be in charge. A little man with a grand sense of self-worth was a dangerous man indeed. Why Surina's father could not see as much was beyond her. She had warned him time and again that Dasin could not be trusted, yet he remained on staff.

He wasn't a good man and seemed to live to torment others. His cruelty to slaves and servants was notorious. On more than one occasion a servant had been lost by his hand, never to be seen again and rumored dead, though he denied the charges leveled against him, each time managing to find favor with her father once more. When she dared to question him about it, her father simply told her that such things were beyond her understanding and her years. She did not see where any amount of age would make Dasin any more appealing.

"You are a filthy dog," Dasin spat, his venomous voice causing a chill to race up her spine. "Unfit to serve here even as a slave."

Surina tensed. If there was one thing she could choose to change about her father it was his keeping of slaves. She was appalled by the practice and always had been. It was the way of her people she was told time and time again. Taking another's freedoms and forcing them into a life of servitude was no *way* in her opinion, but her progressive views were laughed at in social circles and dismissed as a foolish young woman's notions.

The slaves within her father's household said he was a kind and merciful master. One they preferred over others. She imagined they'd rather have freedom than mercy.

The cracking of a whip caused her to jolt and she knew she could no longer remain hidden among the greenery. Not with Dasin unrestricted. She pushed through the opening and came to a grinding halt when she spotted a naked man there, bent on one knee, his head down as his shoulders heaved. A jolt of yearning raced through her. She had never felt such a thing for a man before. And this one was hardly in a state to act upon her feelings, not that she would. The aftereffects of tapping into her magik for the scroll must have left her in a state of longing. That had to be it. She was no woman of the world and did not go about panting after a man.

A very naked man.

Fresh, bloody whip marks marred his otherwise perfect skin. His skin, kissed golden from the sun, glistened with sweat and welling blood. His long, wavy, dark-brown hair hung forward, blocking her view of his face.

For a moment, her gaze drifted to his hip and the side of his ass cheek that was visible from her position. Gripping the scroll tighter, she nearly crushed the parchment. The man was sculpted as though he were a man who knew his way around an arena. She didn't instantly recognize him from the games, though that wasn't surprising. She detested the games, and when she was required to attend, she did her best to focus on anything but the carnage that went on in the arena.

Chains bound his wrists, ankles and neck. The sight of him, surrounded by Dasin and the men loyal to him, sickened her.

She gasped as Dasin lifted the whip again, ready to strike. He spun to face her, his grey eyes wild. "Surina," he purred, the hair on the back of her neck rising at the sound of his voice.

She squared her shoulders, her long, jet-black hair falling over one as she attempted to harden her nerves. "What is the meaning of this?"

He caressed his whip in a sexual manner as his men leered, licking their lips at her. Being anywhere near them all, alone, was unwise. Surina knew as much, but leaving their new play toy to fend for himself wasn't a possibility. Already he was hurt. If left alone with them any longer, he could end up dead.

Even with her somewhat limited skills in the healing arts, she knew his wounds could fester and cause a fever or death if not properly tended to.

"This slave was unruly," Dasin responded, "and needed to be taught a lesson."

"Unruly how?" she demanded, never wavering.

A challenge lit in his eyes. "He refuses to wear the collar or the attire provided for him."

She noticed then the silver collar cast to the side of the naked man. To its right was dingy white material that was used by the males of her kind as an undergarment wrap of sorts. While the guards and others wore additional articles of clothing above it, the slaves were not permitted as much. It kept them from trying to escape into the elements and from stealing, the theory being they could not take what they had no place to hide. She did not see any of them as thieves. She saw them as victims of a cruel society and backwards thinking.

She held Dasin's gaze. "And that has warranted this? Eight men gathered around him, laughing and carrying on while another whips him as though he were an animal?"

Dasin's expression hardened. "He *is* an animal. He is Katarian."

She stiffened, her gaze snapping again to the collar. She knew much of the Katarian. More than she should. She knew silver burned their bare skin to the point the silver would often melt through it. The chains he was currently in were cast from iron. It was the only good point she could find in the situation.

Squaring her shoulders, Surina glared at the guards. "You," she said to one of them, "go to the training facility and fetch the healer. And you," she said to another, "go and select one of the darker collars. Is it not clear this one is too small? Why would he willingly put one on that will choke the breath from him? Can you not see his neck is thick? A dead slave is worth nothing. And what of my father's coin that was used to purchase him? Who will see to it my father is reimbursed?"

If she dared to tell them the man was allergic to silver, they would use the knowledge at a later date to torture him more. "And you," she said to Dasin. "You may report to Lectur. Have you not evening rounds to attend to? Certainly they are more pressing than you overseeing a slave. Such a task is beneath you, is it not?"

The men watched Dasin closely for instruction.

Dasin stiffened. "Dear Surina, to leave you alone with an animal such as this would be unwise. My duty, *as always*, is to protect you."

"Your duty is to obey, or do you forget as much?" she returned, holding her head high, trying to play the part she'd been born to.

"Surina?" a deep voice called from behind her. "When I get my hands on you..."

Rawlin, the head of her personal guard, broke through the opening. His long dark hair was disheveled and his normally perfectly positioned red cloak was cocked to one side. Stray twigs and leaves stuck to both his hair and his cloak. It was then she realized he'd gone to the mazes first, assuming her there, only to get lost himself—again.

Oh, he would be angry for sure.

She couldn't help but instantly compare him to the man on his knees. She'd always thought Rawlin quite striking, and while he still was, the man on his knees was more so. The newcomer made her body tingle with wanton thoughts in addition to a strange level of concern. She was not without heart. Often it was pointed out she cared too much for others, but this was different. She did not just care about this man's well-being. She felt herself becoming obsessed by it.

When Rawlin spotted Dasin, his hand went to the hilt of the sword at his side, worn as all guards of Tamonius did—hung through a metal loop around his corded waist. His green gaze narrowed in suspicion. His mistrust of Dasin was well known.

Dasin tensed and plastered a smile to his face. "Rawlin, I was just scolding Surina for wishing to be alone with this barbarian from the north."

Rawlin didn't comment, but she knew he would at a later date. He found great joy in lecturing her on any and all occasions.

"And I was just informing Dasin he was to report to Lectur at once," she replied. As Lectur was highest in command among the everyday guards, Dasin would be hard pressed to defy him openly. Surina had known Lectur a long time and knew he would hold Dasin's head in his hand before he tolerated disobedience.

Dasin inclined his head. "As you wish, my lady."

He and his men dispersed quickly, but not before they each glared at the man on his knees. Rawlin stayed close. After several tension-filled moments passed, he exhaled. "They are gone from hearing range, Surina. What is the meaning of this?"

She reacted quickly, trying to rush to the man on his knees.

Rawlin caught her arm. "Are you mad? He could break your neck. And he is not properly clothed. Avert your gaze. You are too young to look upon a man wearing naught but what he was born in."

"Please, Rawlin." She struggled to free herself. "He is hurt and he needs assistance. What kind of person would I be to deny help? He is of the Katarian and refused to wear the silver collar. Because he wished not to have his head melted from his very shoulders, Dasin took it as a direct challenge. He is an evil man. One you swore to me would be sent away. Why is he still here? One such as he should not be permitted near anyone, let alone those who cannot defend themselves."

"He currently holds your father's favor. Or worse, he holds something over your father's head. Something that your father finds himself having to bend over again and again." Rawlin sighed, his gaze going to the man on the ground. "Surina, the rest of the guard unit

29

assigned to you searches for you. Go and find them. Tell them I am here. They will assist in carrying the slave to the healing chambers."

"The man." She pushed on her longtime friend's chest. "Not the slave. He is a man. Or do you so quickly forget that fact? Are you too like Dasin?"

Rawlin released his hold on her. "Surina, no. You know I am not."

She bolted to the man on the ground and grabbed the cloth. When the smell of urine caught her attention, she knew then that Dasin had done as she'd heard of him doing before—he'd ordered his men to piss upon the cloth. It was yet another way they attempted to humiliate the slaves brought in.

Sickened, she cast it aside and removed her *palla*. She was left in nothing more than a thin tunic. The enchanted scroll fell to the ground before she could think to hide the contraband story. She made of point of paying no mind to it, hoping Rawlin would do the same. Rawlin gasped at the sight of her in nothing but her tunic. That was fine by her. If his attention was on her it was not upon the scroll.

She edged closer to the man on the ground. "Sir," she said in his native tongue, enjoying getting to use it once more. It had been weeks since her last brush with it. She greatly missed talking with Jaelyn and getting to explore another way of things. "Please. I know you have no reason to trust me and that you could, should you wish, remove my head with ease, but please, my intent is only to aid you."

He lifted his head, his brown gaze piercing her very soul. He was striking—his features chiseled, hard, all male. Her body lit with need and she had to concentrate on her breathing. Already she lost the battle with her cheeks as they flared with pink.

"You speak with the tongue of Katarius, yet you are not of our kind. You are not Katarian," he said, his voice deep, reverberating through her.

Rawlin was close, his sword at the ready.

She held a hand up. "No."

"What does he say to you?" Rawlin demanded. "Does he speak harsh words?"

She hid her smile. "No. He speaks with a civil tongue. Please, step back. His experience with those who wear the red has not been good. I wish not for him to associate it with danger any longer. He requires healing attention, a bath, a hot meal and rest." She glanced at the collar. "Rawlin, can you see to it he's not put in anything silver?"

"Surina?" Rawlin asked.

"For me. Please."

She reached out with a tentative hand, holding the material of her *palla* to the man, keeping her gaze from wandering over parts of him it should not. "Here. I would cover you myself, but I know the Katarian have a different way than we of how it is they cover themselves," she said in his language. "I also know that the rumors of you all running about nude are greatly exaggerated. Please—" She held the cloth out more to him. "—it is clean, of this I assure you. It has touched only my body. Though, with your heightened senses, I imagine you already know as much."

"Surina," Rawlin injected. He bent and retrieved the crushed scroll from the ground. Her heart hammered in her chest. Surina tensed but Rawlin merely lifted it towards her. "Take your etiquette scroll back to your bedroom."

Etiquette scroll?

She glanced at it and realized it did bear markings similar to those used for etiquette scrolls.

"Seek out the others," Rawlin said. "I will see to this slave's, *erm,* man's needs."

"Thank you, Rawlin. You are a good man." She took the scroll, glad its contents had not been discovered.

Chapter Three

Kritan narrowed his gaze on the female before him as she clutched the scroll to her chest. His body was battered, bruised and bloody, yet all he could focus upon was her. Her scent assailed him, making him dizzy with need. When she'd arrived and he'd first caught her aroma, and the sweet scent of her sex, it had been all he could do to stay semi-upright. The smell of her cream was divine and he wanted it on his tongue. He wanted it rubbed all over his cock. But there was more. A strange attraction to her that had nothing to do with his dick and everything to do with something else—something Kritan did not yet want to think further upon.

Grab her. Claim her.

The powerful urge to obey his inner beast was nearly crippling. He had to grit his teeth and dig his nails into the palms of his hands to keep from doing exactly what he wished to do. It took a moment for him to calm himself enough to think beyond grunts and growls.

Upon looking at her, her beauty managed to exceed his expectations. Long, black hair hung to her slim waist, accentuating her curves. Wide eyes, as green as the leaves of summer in Katarius, stared up at him. They were rimmed with thick, dark eyelashes. And her lips, they were full, subtle, berry-colored and tempting unlike any other he'd laid witness too.

He quaked with the compulsion to kiss her, to taste of her mouth and then bury his face in her cunt. Never had a woman caused such an outlandish reaction in him. He was known for his ability to coax the females to his bed with ease. He was equally known for being absent from said bed come morning light, but this one—this female— he could see himself remaining in place for. He could see himself wrapping his body around hers to ensure she was still with him come morning.

33

Absurd!

He was a king. He did not long to hold anyone.

Did he?

The more he looked upon the beauty, the more he had his answer. For he more than wanted to simply hold her. He wanted to grab her to him and never release her. She could be his captive and he knew he'd never tire of her.

She was tall, yet nowhere near his height. Her breasts were smaller than he normally preferred, but plenty enough to fill his hands. It was easy to imagine her minus her tunic, her nipples in his mouth as he ran his hands over her body. Women should not come as tempting as she, for it would be commonplace for kings to hand over countries should the woman simply request it.

"Please," she repeated in his native tongue. Her accurate pronunciation surprised him. "Take the cloth. I know that contrary to what others think, you do not wish to be nude for all to see."

The shifters of his race did not view nudity as something to be ashamed of. But she was right; they did not constantly walk about naked for all to look upon. They tended to save such things for full moons when they would shift and run wild, then gather for food, drink and sex. Not all within the kingdom of Katarius could shift forms. Some were magiks of varying levels, while some possessed no gifts—they were merely mortal.

He eyed her closely, wondering where her knowledge came from. He did believe it something taught to the youth of Tamonius. If anything, they were probably told the Katarian lifted their legs to piss and fucked cattle. He'd heard rumors of certain falsehoods about his kind—ones saying the shifters of his race simply stole the women they wanted, fucked them and then disposed of the bodies. "How is it you know so much of my kind? Are you not fearful I will steal you away,

34

force myself upon you before putting you on a spit and dining on your flesh?"

She offered a smile and Kritan fought desperately to keep from reaching out and touching her. The idea of stealing her away actually sounded like a good one. The guard who was protective of her would react if Kritan so much as laid a hand upon her, even if just to see if her skin was as smooth as it appeared to be.

If Kritan was right, the guard was more than merely protective. He had not missed the smell of the guard's arousal upon seeing the woman.

"Sir, I do not believe for a moment you will steal me away or attempt to have your way with me. For I know the Katarian are not as campfire stories make them out to be. And you are not cannibals, so you can stop with your attempts to shock and scare me. I am not a child nor do I fear childhood stories. I am a woman and I will not permit you to be treated in such a manner as I found again."

Already Kritan had been beaten, starved and tortured by those of their kind—the Tamoni. It had been weeks since he'd found himself ambushed by the enemy in the Den of Debauchery, only to awaken shackled. His captors did not understand who they held. They thought him a mere foot soldier in the Katarian army.

Fools.

When it had become clear that no amount of torture would make him talk, they had taken him to auction. He had been bought and brought here, with the idea he would fight in the games. He was a strong man. Breaking his spirit and his body was not an easy feat. As of yet, the Tamoni had not managed to do so.

The woman edged closer to him. She was foolish to trust him. He could kill her in the blink of an eye, but the very idea nearly did what Dasin and the others could not. It nearly broke him. No harm would come to her. Not from his hand or any other. He and his beast agreed.

Her hand grazed his upper arm and the action caused his cock to harden rapidly. Hell yes, she was indeed a woman, not a child. His body recognized as much. So did he. He winced, keeping his body positioned in a way he hoped kept the sight of his erection hidden from her. No need to permit her knowledge of the power she seemed to have over him. A part of him wondered if she was gifted with magiks of seduction. Perhaps that was how she had enticed him so quickly and so completely by doing nothing more than looking at him.

No. While he smelled hints of magik upon her, he did not detect a spell at work. There was no trickery at play. Only raw animal attraction that he suffered from in waves that nearly crippled him.

Her gaze never moved from his face and he knew then she was going out of her way to avoid looking upon his nude form. The thought nearly brought a smile to his lips. It meant she was indeed a lady—not one of the Tamoni women he heard so much about, and who he'd gotten a glimpse of in Vesta. The ones who were totally and completely free with their desires and demands. While he enjoyed a woman who could fuck, he didn't want the beauty before him to be worldly in such ways. He wanted to believe she had limited experiences in regards to males.

Surina.

The name the others called her by was as beautiful as she.

She eased even closer to him, her gaze going to his shoulder and upper back. Her lips drew tight and her eyes moistened. "You have need of a healer. Your wounds from the whip are deep. Should they not have healed over on their own already? I was told the Katarian heal at a rate much faster than the Tamoni."

Normally, that would be the case, but he was not at full strength at the moment. The worry upon her face ripped at his gut. He found himself reaching out to touch her. Her guard reacted, seeing the action as a threat to the woman. The guard kicked Kritan in the chest, knocking him off balance and away from Surina.

Surina screamed, and the next thing Kritan knew, her body was coming down over him. She shielded him from any more blows, her body lying on his. "Rawlin, no!"

"Surina, up, this instant," the guard shouted. There was no mistaking the jealous tone in his voice. Kritan had been right; the guard felt something more than simply the need to protect the woman.

He fought a growl, jealous himself.

Kritan continued to hide the fact he spoke fluent Tamoni. He remained perfectly still, knowing if he dared to move with her upon him, he'd likely grab hold of her hips and drive himself far into her cunt. She was wet. He could smell as much and the scent was glorious. One he wished to bury his face in for all his days. If he was not careful, he'd find himself laying claim to the beauty. Explaining her to his kingdom would be difficult or impossible.

Here is your new queen—a Tamoni.

She eased up slowly at first, straddling his waist as a lover would. He flashed an arrogant smile in the direction of the guard, one the woman could not see. She seemed oblivious to her actions upon him, and what it did to him, her focus on her guard. "He was not trying to harm me. I think he simply wished to touch me."

"Unacceptable," Rawlin said, his voice clipped and his posture rigid. "Get off him this instant. He is nude and you are in naught more than a thin tunic. Already you ride astride him in a way not of my liking. Give me not more reason to be his end, for at this moment I would like nothing more."

Surina's brow knit a half second before she glanced down at Kritan, her gaze widening as if she had only just understood her position upon him. "Oh, I, umm, oh."

She scampered off him like a scared, tiny animal, brushing past his cock on the way. She yelped and slipped to her side, hitting the ground hard. Kritan reacted, moving with his normal speed, grabbing her and pulling her to her knees before him. He dusted off her side and removed bits of grass from her hair before running his forefinger over her smooth cheek.

She swallowed hard. "Thank you, but we should worry more of you than me. You are injured. I am merely clumsy and such a thing happens all the time." She reddened. "Well, not this type of thing. I mean I do trip often or walk into objects, not men's shafts...erm, I mean..." Her face was a bright crimson. "I do not fall upon naked men all the time," she said in his tongue.

Good thing she did not make a habit of lying upon naked men, because Kritan suddenly had the urge to kill any who dared touch her in such a way.

She batted her eyelashes "I am embarrassed now. My apologies. I meant you no disrespect and it was not my intent to take liberties with you, sir. I only wished to stop Rawlin from striking you again."

"No offense was offered, so none can be taken," he said softly, amused greatly by her antics. Her explanation, innocent at its heart, was a stark contrast to the Vesta whores he'd encountered.

She motioned to the markings upon his upper arm. "I am not very good at reading your language. I fear I spent more time daydreaming rather than listening to the one who instructed me on such. I do know the Katarian have such markings placed upon them when they tie themselves to another—um, we refer to it as marriage, but I know you call it something different."

Her knowledge of their kind continued to surprise Kritan. He inclined his head. "It is true. A brand appears on a male's skin to announce to all that he has mated. That he and his mate have bonded."

A strange sadness settled over her that she attempted to mask from him with a smile pressed to her beautiful face, but he detected the truth easily enough. "Again, I am sorry for having climbed atop you in such a manner. I think the offense was against your wife as much as you. Forgive me."

She believed him mated.

He tipped his head, keeping the guard in his sights as he watched Surina. She was young, but more than old enough to be of mating age—especially by the kingdom's low standards.

He snorted. If going by the standards of Tamonius, she was much past the point to marry.

Wretched place.

He entertained allowing her to think what she may of his markings, but something deep within would not permit her sadness to continue. "I am not mated," he revealed, telling her more in the few minutes he'd known her than he had to the guards who had held him captive for nearly two weeks.

Curiously, she cast a sideways glance at his arm. "But you wear the band on your arm."

"My *left* arm," he corrected, unsure why he felt compelled to tutor her on the ways of his people. "When one finds and claims his lifemate, it is his right arm that the brands appear upon."

Her brows drew together in deep thought and he nearly laughed despite his situation. "They appear?"

He nodded. "They do."

"So you have magik?"

Kritan's lips twitched. "To a certain degree. Nowhere near what the highborns here have."

"Interesting." She tipped her head, still focusing on his arms. "And the left?" she inquired. "Why does one mark it in such a manner?"

39

"To tell of one's position within Katarius. And no one does it to themselves. They appear as well, first at birth and then at random throughout life," he said, surprising himself with just how open and honest he was being with her. It was unwise to reveal all to her no matter how much she made his loins stir. Despite her kindness to him and her knowledge of his kind, she was still, technically, the enemy. But a beautiful enemy, for sure. "Mine speak of being a warrior."

Not a lie. Not the total truth either. Telling the timeline of his life, in order they labeled him first a noble, of the highest royal blood, next a prince, and then the third spoke of his ascent to king. The remaining markings told of his skills as a warrior of the highest degree.

"Surina, end this with him now," Rawlin said, agitated. "I will see him to the slave quarters. The healer may visit him there. You've no place around him any longer. You have done as you set out to do. You stopped Dasin and his men from further harming the man. You must return to the main house, bathe and prepare yourself for dinner, or do you forget Lord Wysely arrives on this night to feast with you?"

She curled her lip. "He arrives to undress me with his eyes while he shovels food into his fat face. He is a stain on society." She shuddered. "I spend the entire time at the dinner hoping he chokes upon the bones of the animal he pushes into his mouth."

Kritan licked his lips, trying and nearly failing to keep from smiling. On one hand he found her attitude on the matter amusing. On the other he wanted to snap this Lord Wysely's neck.

A tic started in the guard's jaw. "I know he is not to your liking, but he is a very rich man, Surina. He could provide a very comfortable life for you. He is a nobleman and you are a noblewoman. The match could work well."

Kritan knew they assumed he did not understand their language, or else they would not speak so freely in front of him—a slave. The guards who had captured him had made many failed attempts at his language, thinking him unable to speak their own.

Listening closer, he kept his face devoid of emotion. He did not, as of yet, want to tip his hand.

"No amount of money in the world could prompt me to want that within me—siring sons upon me. No way. No how." She jerked her chin up defiantly.

Rawlin snickered and quickly wiped the smirk away. "But, Surina. He is one of the few men your father permits to continue to try to court you."

"My father does no such thing," Surina snapped, her temper showing. "He humors the spoiled brat because he is his godfather. Father has stressed on numerous occasions that he would rather I devote my life in service of the gods, never bearing him a grandchild, than be with one such as Wysely. He thinks of him not in terms of a man but as something on the lines of excrement."

Rawlin coughed to hide his laugh, clearly toying with her. "I see, and do you share your father's view?"

"No. I think he stops shy of all Wysely truly is. But for me to repeat them would make your ears turn red, so I will resist." A sly smile spread over her face. "Rawlin, order the flags to be raised—the ones saying sickness has arrived at the estate."

Rawlin quirked a brow. "Surina?"

"Wysely fears illness in the worst way. He was sickly as a child and always believes himself afflicted with this ailment or that. And if he and his riding party should spot the flags…"

Rawlin tossed his head back and laughed. "He will refuse to join you for dinner and will insist they return to his home."

She smiled. "Yes."

41

"Is your father aware of just how strangely your mind works?" he asked.

She shrugged. The scroll she seemed protective of fell to the ground once more, this time rolling open. Kritan could read the written word of Tamonius as well, but not with great ease, not like he could his own language. What he did see caused him to blink several times. He watched as the scroll sprang to life, the ink forming into figures that began to copulate.

Time seemed to tick by, no one moving, no one saying a word. Finally, a weak sound came from Surina as her face stained with color. Rawlin seemed to come out of his stupor, his mouth dropping, his eyes wide. It was all Kritan could do to keep from laughing.

The Tamoni were certainly amusing if nothing else.

Suddenly, Rawlin seized hold of the scroll, his gaze wild and upon Surina. "This is not a scroll of etiquette!"

"I never said it was. You assumed," she said, her voice tiny.

Rawlin fumed. "Surina!"

Surina's face was crimson as she reached unsuccessfully for the scroll. "Rawlin, please."

The guard clutched the scroll and the figures vanished. "You have read this?"

She lowered her gaze. "Yes."

"Why?"

Surina bit at her lower lip. "How else am I to learn of what happens between a man and a woman?"

Rawlin huffed. "You could ask me."

"Ask you?" she questioned, looking horrified at the idea. "I couldn't. I wouldn't."

Rawlin rolled the scroll and put it in the waistband of his tunic. The man cleared his throat and Kritan sensed a lie about to roll from the man's tongue. "This is not the way of things between a man and a woman. This is merely fiction. One does not do these types of things. Ever."

Kritan strongly suspected the guard wanted to do exactly those types of things with Surina. He fought the urge to growl, disliking that idea strongly. The only reason he did not attack the man was because Surina seemed clueless of Rawlin's attraction to her.

Shame was evident on Surina's face and Kritan disliked seeing her in such a state. Kritan eased his hand in her direction, his fingers skimming hers. Her gaze snapped to him. Her breathing quickened and Kritan could smell the changes in her body. She too was attracted to him, though not practiced enough in the art of womanly ways to hide the fact from him. The thought pleased him greatly.

She cleared her throat. "The cloth. Accept it, I beg of you. I know it is not what you are used to, but for the time being it will serve its purpose."

It also smelled of her. He would bury his face in it later as he grasped his cock, pumping to thoughts of her green gaze upon him. He was about to take the material from her when her guard bent and retrieved the silver collar. Kritan growled and Rawlin moved closer to him. It was Surina who reacted, gasping and ripping the collar from the guard's hands.

She held it tightly down towards the ground. Intense pain radiated from her—and Kritan felt it as if it were his own—yet by all outward appearances, she seemed completely fine.

"Rawlin, summon the healer," she whispered. "I beg of you."

"I will not leave you with him!" Rawlin shouted, clearly worked up from the scroll incident still. Kritan guessed the man's hard attitude had something to do with the scroll he'd seen and less to do with his dislike of Kritan. "Go now. You should not be so close to this one, regardless how big your heart is. He is clearly honed from sword fighting and the gods only know what else."

"He will not harm me," she said softly, her hands starting to shake as she hid them from view.

Kritan stared harder at her hands and a sinking feeling came over him.

"You cannot know that," Rawlin returned.

Kritan knocked the collar free from her grasp and it fell to the ground. She stared up at him with tear-soaked eyes, her palms hidden from view. Kritan ignored the guard and his rant as he took hold of her wrists and turned her palms face-up.

There, before him, he saw the truth of why she seemed to know so much of his kind—deep, angry blisters and burns on her palms in the exact shape of the collar.

Kritan gasped. "You? You have the blood of the Katarian in you?"

She did not respond to him. Instead, she looked towards Rawlin. "He will not harm me."

"Surina," Rawlin protested.

"Do you wish me to beg?" she asked. "I will."

"It is my sworn duty to protect you," Rawlin said. "I have watched over you since you were but a child. To ask me to walk away, to turn my back upon a warrior who, I have no doubt, can and will harm you, is too much. Your heart is big. Bigger than your head at times. You cannot save them all, and to try to do so with this slave is foolish. It will cost you your life."

Kritan lifted the cloth before him—the one she had given him. He set about wrapping it around himself in a way that left his lower portion covered fully. He lifted his head, his gaze going to Rawlin. "If I wished

44

her dead," he said in their language with only the slightest touch of an accent, "she would be. She has been the only light I have seen in this forsaken country, and to extinguish such a light is not within me. She requires the aid of this healer she wishes you to summon. Do so at once."

It was Surina's turn to draw in a deep breath. "You speak Tamoni?"

He inclined his head slightly. "I found no reason to dignify the others with a response."

Rawlin eyes him suspiciously.

Kritan snorted. "No fear, your secrets are safe with me."

"I could cut your tongue out. That would assure you do not speak," Rawlin said, touching the hilt of his sword.

Surina gasped.

Rawlin tempered his expression as he looked to Kritan. "Can you walk?"

Kritan nodded and tried to stand. Surina reacted quickly, standing as well, putting her body to his to try to help as much as possible. Her offer did not go unnoticed by Kritan. He inhaled deeply, her head just shy of his chin, her hair smelling of flowers.

Rawlin attempted to assist as well and Kritan growled.

Surina ran her palm over his smooth chest. "I trust him fully. He is not as Dasin is. He is not cruel of the heart."

But he wants you and that is unacceptable to me.

Kritan held his tongue.

Rawlin caught her wrist and lifted her hand, his gaze upon the burn marks on her palm. "Surina, what happened? This is fresh. How?" He looked towards the collar and sucked in a huge breath. "The silver. It affects you as it would them. How can that be? Your mother, she was only half Katarian. And I have known you a long time; you did not have issue with silver when you were a child." He stilled, releasing her hand. "I remember your mother asking me to give you a tiny silver bracelet she wished you to have. I knew not then the truth of the harm it could cause a Katarian. Had I known, I would have never given it to you."

"It hurt me not then, Rawlin," she said. "I believe it was her way to hide the truth of what I am. Her sensitivity to it was low so she thought I would have little to none. While young, I did not."

"Yet silver, on this day, has caused you great injury," Rawlin returned, concern in his voice.

She took a deep breath. "I am fine. Let us worry of our guest. He has suffered more than I could even begin to think upon."

"Our guest?" Rawlin asked. "Surina, do not get it into your head that you can free him. You know it cannot be done. You have tried before and failed."

"I know no such thing." She turned, her hand going to Kritan's chest.

Kritan stared down at her. Even now, knowing Kritan understood the guard's tongue, Rawlin talked around him as if he were not there. Or not of consequence. The act showed how little the guard thought of a slave. "Do nothing that will cause you harm or anger those in charge. I wish not for you to be hurt for me."

She grinned slightly. "And I wish not for you to hurt. Let us see whose will is stronger?"

He'd not met a woman such as her before. She was both tender and innocent and crafty and cunning all at once. It was alluring, to say the least.

"I will see him to the slave quarters and bring the healer to him. If you swear to me you will part with us and go directly to the main house and seek assistance for your hands," Rawlin said. "Tell them you were burned by an oil lamp. Do not reveal the truth, regardless how much a friend you think them. Surina, a friend can quickly become an enemy. Do you swear?"

"I swear," she answered fast.

Kritan turned, permitting the man to assist him. He glanced at Surina and winked. She gasped and stepped back from him before doing the most curious of things—she looked behind her as if she expected to find another he'd winked at.

"Kritan," he said.

She lifted a brow in question.

"My name," he offered, "is Kritan."

"You've the same name as the King of Katarian?"

He nodded. "I do. It is not that uncommon of a name."

Lie.

Chapter Four

Rawlin, Head Guard to Daughter of Argyros and High Magik Legionnaire Knight of the First Order, watched as Surina headed back in the direction of the main house. The sway of her hips was tempting, as always. He pushed his magik out, alerting the guards beneath him that she was unescorted. They should have never let her wander off on her own as it was. He'd have words with them later. Rawlin had a sneaking suspicion Surina had cast a spell of her own to ensure herself a private moment. He knew how much she valued solitude, how much she enjoyed time to think without the watchful eyes of guards on her.

While the country estate was normally a safe haven for her, change was afoot. Whispers of rebellion had spread and Argyros had gone to the capital city of Unus in hopes of dispelling the rumors. Already, peace within Tamonius was held together by threads—ones that were worn and stretched to the breaking point. It was not a safe time for travel and one never knew whom one could trust. Rawlin hoped Argyros's contacts in Unus were dependable. If not, Argyros was walking into a trap and Surina would be without a father. Having no husband or brother, she was not permitted to inherit Argyros's estate or position in the senate.

If Rawlin's fears came true and Argyros did not survive the stirrings of unrest in Unus, Rawlin had sworn an oath to the man. He would force Surina's hand in marriage. Rawlin would wed her and protect her—keeping Argyros's estates and position from falling into the hands of the enemy, and more importantly, keep his daughter from ending up a pawn in an age-old game. A document, proclaiming an officially decreed marriage between Rawlin and Surina, was signed and hidden safely in the main house, should the unthinkable come to pass.

Yes, the document was falsified, but it would not matter.

Rawlin exhaled, the tensions of the day eating at him. Surina would not be the same without her father. She loved him greatly and Argyros showered her in love and gifts, doing his best to shelter her from the ugliness that Tamonius had become.

Senators worried more about power and less about the state of things. It had been this way for some time, making Tamonius a good place to simply arrive and then fade away. For one such as himself, it was exactly what he'd needed. A place where everyone was more concerned with themselves than others. A place he would not be noticed for who and what he truly was.

He laughed to himself.

He had hardly faded away into oblivion as he'd hoped to do. He had found a friend in Argyros. And friendship had a way of coming back to bite one on the backside.

When Rawlin was sure Surina was to safety and guarded by men he trusted, he rounded on the beast man. The damned Katarian's arrival could not have come at a worse time. Already Rawlin was on edge, fearing word would reach him of something horrible happening to Argyros. Too long had passed since a missive had arrived telling of the progress happening in Unus. Jaelyn, Argyros's head guard and trusted friend to Rawlin, had sent no updates for nearly two full weeks.

Rawlin did not need another worry, another hassle. It would be all too easy for him to allow even a tiny portion of his true power to rise and end the Katarian. End the extra stress at an already stress-laden time.

"You reek of want for her," he snapped, slow-burning anger reflected in his eyes. He disliked Surina's interest in the newcomer.

Kritan looked him up and down, arching an impervious brow. "As do you."

True enough.

Rawlin was conflicted over his feelings for Surina. While she was young he'd been protective of her. When she reached womanhood, his feelings had begun to change, evolving into something more. Something even he had yet to completely come to terms with. He had not acted on his desires for her out of respect for her father and because he didn't feel she was ready for more. And he disliked the idea of making her a secret lover and using her to sate his daily needs.

As a magik of the highest order, sex wasn't a luxury, it was a requirement. He'd bedded more women than he could ever begin to recall. He had been alive far too long to form pointless attachments such as love, yet if he were pressed to label what he felt for Surina it would fall in that direction. Even if he didn't subscribe to love, he did want her, and he sure as hell didn't want her touched by the Katarian. A deep churning in his gut told him that no matter the obstacle he set between Surina and the beast slave, the two would come together and join. Jealousy coursed through his veins. However, if he were to end the Katarian's life, Surina would never forgive him.

Something Rawlin couldn't live with.

He'd not thought Surina ready for such feelings, such desires. Seeing the scroll she'd been hiding, he knew better. She was far more than ready. And now her interests were on the newcomer—the beast man. Rawlin could sense the attraction she held for Kritan. He wanted to deny the truth of the matter, but couldn't. It was as if deep magik was at play.

Destiny.

He curled his lip, his dislike of destiny great. He'd been avoiding his own so long he'd thought himself clear of it.

Apparently not.

Rawlin thought of the marriage decree hidden away and touched the scroll in his waistband. He turned his attention on Kritan. "Come. I made an oath to Surina to see you to the healer and I will do as much. I do not break my word to her."

Kritan smirked. "Died a little inside when you swore the oath to her, didn't you?"

"Since I am the only one here on your side, not counting Surina, you might try a little less mockery and a little more appreciation," Rawlin reminded the beast man.

Kritan lifted his shoulders, letting them fall swiftly, suggesting he didn't care if he had allies. Rawlin had seen men like him over the course of his immortally long life. There was something in Kritan's posture and his gaze that said he was a man of power. A man who normally demanded a great deal of respect. What Rawlin couldn't figure out was how the man had ended up in chains, or why it was Surina had seemed so instantly attracted to him—and he to her.

You know why. You simply choose to ignore it.

He winced, wanting to silence his inner voice. It had been torturing him for centuries.

If all ended well with Argyros and Jaelyn and their visit to Unus, Rawlin would ask Jaelyn what he knew of Kritan. After all, Jaelyn hailed from Katarius and was of the same race of beast men. Rawlin led Kritan through the gardens in the direction of the slave quarters. As they passed the training yard, Kritan slowed, paying close attention to the men conditioning for the arena games.

Rawlin had long ago desensitized himself to the ugly side of life on Panucia. Besides, he had seen worse. He had been alive during the times of space travel—of exploring other universes and planets. A time when all of Panucia had been seen as gods as they spread across the galaxies. Rawlin remembered his time on Earth as if it were yesterday.

Mars.

The name seemed foolish to him then. It was what the humans of Earth had labeled him. Others like himself from Panucia had been given similarly outlandish names and worshiped for one thing or another.

The god of war.

He shuddered.

For centuries he'd been outrunning his past, outrunning the death and destruction that seemed to follow in his wake. Yet he never seemed to be able to run far enough.

You are death. Admit it.

Rawlin had to nudge Kritan to get him to move in the direction of the healer's quarters. He strongly suspected the man had already begun to hatch plans of a rebellion in his head. He seemed the type. Rawlin wasn't in the mood to deal with pathetic attempts at freedom. He had bigger things to worry himself with.

This one will make it a concern, he thought to himself. *Perhaps I should allow him to escape. Surina would be satisfied if he found freedom rather than an arena.*

Honor forbade going through with the thought, though it was a good one.

As he walked, Rawlin noted the old, faded scars upon Kritan's back. He'd not noticed them at first because of the fresh, bloody whip marks. Whoever the man was, he had seen battle. That much was easy to tell.

The healer's quarters were close to the slave lodgings. It was a wise move on Argyros's part, for most of the injuries and sickness occurred among the slaves. Argyros, like all senators in Tamonius, was required to enter gladiators into arena games. The times Argyros had tried to take a stand by refusing to send men to fight had each been met with raids upon Argyros's various estates. Surina had been harmed in one of the so-called random raids. After that, Argyros did not refuse to send men to fight. Instead, he bought the best fighters he could find, trained them and treated them well, assuring they wanted to fight, and he promised them freedom should they win enough battles. Argyros held true to his promises and had already given notes of freedom to at least a half dozen of the slaves who had once fought for him. Considering how hard notes of freedom were to come by in Tamonius, that was saying something. It also angered the nobles.

Something Argyros loved to do.

When they reached the healer's quarters, Rawlin motioned to two of the guards to come to him. He nudged Kritan, who growled in response. "See to it Yusoni is summoned and that he treats this one's wounds. Have this man fed and then see to it he rests. Surina's orders."

The guards shared a confused look but nodded. They would obey. He knew the men and knew they did not follow the ways of Dasin. They were loyal to Argyros. Kritan would be seen to as Surina had wished.

Rawlin left the beast man in the care of the guards and wasted no time covering the estate grounds to return to the main house. He went directly to his chambers. He removed his red cloak, casting it aside as he took the scroll from his waistband. He tapped it, his magik initiating the enchantment.

Rawlin observed in quiet reserve as the scroll played out an erotic love story. The figures began by orally pleasing one another and then moved to a standard joining before the male took the female from behind. So this was what Surina wanted? She wanted a man to take her, claim her like an animal and fuck every inch of her.

Interesting.

He would have never have guessed her wild and wanting.

Fuck, his cock was hard.

He was capable of giving her such things and more. The idea of acting out the scroll with her stirred his cock. No surprise there. His line of magiks required sex. He often sought out several of the servant girls who attended to Surina. They enjoyed sex and seemed pleased to have his attentions. They fucked well enough but he desired more. Something they could never give him. They were not his true mate. Therefore, he could never fully form a bond with any of them and he could never find rest from the wicked in their arms.

No. That curse had been laid upon him long ago.

He pulled off his tunic and tossed it onto his bed, his gaze remaining on the scroll. There was a knock on his chamber door. He tipped his head. "What?"

"Sir, the cook has sent food. She says you have not eaten today," Lucila, a house servant and handmaiden to Surina, called out from the other side of the door.

Rawlin's lips curved upwards. Perfect timing. Lucila would work nicely to help alleviate the heaviness in his ball sac. "Enter."

She opened the door, a tray of food and drink in hand. Her brown eyes widened at the sight of him naked, but the surprise was quickly replaced with desire. He knew her sexual tells. The way her left shoulder lowered as a sly smile touched her lips before she would rock to one side and then the other, watching him the entire time. He'd fucked her enough to spot the signs with ease and she did them all now. She entered the room fully and shut the door before setting the food and drink on the table. She stood at attention, her coy gaze moving slightly to the scroll that was still playing out its erotic scenes.

"Come," Rawlin motioned to her. "Do you wish to view it more closely?"

She swallowed hard. "I already have, sir."

He'd suspected as much. She was close friends to Surina. No doubt the two giggled and watched the scroll's enchantment often. He wondered what else they did with it. "Lucila."

She lifted her chin. "Yes."

"Is there anything else? Beyond the food, that you wish to tell me of?"

She eyed his cock and licked her lower lip. "If you would like, I could tend to you."

Desire rolled off her. She wanted sex. He needed it. Their arrangement worked well. He curved two fingers at her. "Come closer and kneel before me."

A half smile lit her face. She hurried to him and knelt before him, her blonde hair falling forward. Her breasts were smaller than he normally liked and showed as her tunic was only tied loosely at the top. Where Surina stayed fully covered for the most part, the other females on the estate dressed provocatively—as was often the case because of their native kingdoms or planets of origin. Lucila was from the Vamone, to the far northeast of Tamonius. The Vamonie had reputation for being barbarians who would rather pillage than do an honest day's work. He knew that to be a lie.

She was lovely. He'd give her that. And she could fuck well enough. He pushed her hair over her shoulders and stared down at her, seeing that her nipples were hard. "I wish to have my cock sucked and then I will have your pussy. Yes?"

She nodded eagerly.

He did not fear disease or pregnancy. He was an immortal—immune to such sicknesses and unable to impregnate anyone other than his true mate, of which Lucila was not. Rawlin had given up on the idea of ever finding his true mate. The idea was nearly laughable. After all, he had been alive for centuries with no sign of her. He had resigned himself to being forever cursed, doomed to walk the planet, paying for the sins of his past, never knowing true love.

Such was the way of things.

His magik had been used to place spells over the wombs of the female servants. They would not conceive a child while the spell lasted. Every two years he performed the spells again on each the female slaves.

Children born from a slave had almost no chance of a good life. Within the walls of the House of Argyros they would not be slaughtered, as in most houses in Tamonius. But they could not remain either. That was why Argyros had asked Rawlin to do such a spell. He knew what the orphanages were like in Tamonius. If the children lived to be ten summers, they would be taken to auction and sold to the highest bidder.

Lucila took hold of Rawlin's shaft and stroked it, her delicate fingers encouraging the blood flow to it more. She leaned, her tongue darting out and over the tip of his cock. Such a sight to behold. She fluttered her tongue over his slit, causing the muscles in his thighs to tighten. She knew what he liked.

She added her hands, stroking his cock and cupping his ball sac. He touched her lower lip, pulling her mouth open more. He pushed the head of his cock into her mouth and she eased over him, taking him deep. Rawlin tipped his head back, his thoughts going to Surina. Now that he knew she was sexually curious, he couldn't help but think of her being in front of him, of her mouth on his dick.

For now, Lucila would have to do.

Taking hold of the sides of her head, Rawlin looked down upon her as she face-fucked him. Her hot, wet mouth sucked sweetly on his cock as she stimulated his sac. He pumped in and out. She relaxed her jaw, letting him go balls deep—the way he liked it. He moved at a leisurely pace, enjoying the pleasure she gave him. He knew she wanted more, so he allowed his magik to rise. It eased over her, caressing her body tenderly, erotically. His magik concentrated on her breasts at first and then slid lower, going for her cunt. She sucked harder on him as his magik eased in and out of her pussy.

Rawlin pulled free of Lucila's mouth and reached down, jerking her up and to her feet. He lifted her with ease and she wrapped her legs around his waist without question. He thrust into her wet cunt, his mouth finding hers. He drilled into her until he could no longer hold back, his thought going to Surina once more. He wondered what her tight pussy would feel like on his cock. The idea sent him over the edge. He pulled free from Lucila just as her orgasm struck. Rawlin grabbed his cock, holding it as seed erupted from the tip, striking her stomach. He drew her against him, kissing her more, unconcerned with the fact he was now covered in his own seed.

When he felt satisfied, he lowered Lucila to the ground. "My thanks."

"Of course, sir," she breathed, a look of longing in her eyes.

He knew she wanted more from him. She wanted an offer of marriage, but that could not be. He had been open with her from the start. He would fuck her. He would make her come. He would not make her his wife. She and the other females on the estate he used to sate his sex lust had all been told upfront that he would not commit to them.

She adjusted her tunic, a clear semen stain on the front of it. She licked her lower lip, appearing satisfied, as if the stain were a badge of honor. "I must change."

"Go and do so. Thank you for the food."

She glanced up at him. "Will you have need of me later?"

"No," he said, turning his back to her as he headed to the bathing chamber adjacent to his room. It was large and the ceiling was rounded with a skylight in it, helping to illuminate the otherwise dark room. The walls were painted a deep red and the linens surrounding the bathing pool itself were a mix of yellows, oranges and reds. On occasion orgies were held in the room, people lining up on the sides as others filled the water, each person engaged in an act of sex. Rawlin only held such orgies when Surina was not present in the home. Argyros enjoyed the festivities but would not have tolerated them occurring while his daughter was in residence.

Rawlin snorted. If the man had any idea about the scroll, he would make Rawlin construct a room of magik that Surina could not leave.

Such an overprotective father.

Descending the steps, Rawlin relaxed, wading deeper into the large pool of natural spring water. The main house boasted several bathing chambers. The slave quarters had one and the healer's quarters had a small one. It was not as grand as the home he'd been raised in, but was grand all the same.

The hot water washed away his seed and the soreness in his muscles from tension. He lost himself in thought for a time, relaxing, letting the worries of the day wash away. When done, Rawlin stepped out of the bathing pool and felt magik nearing. Closing his eyes, he focused, sensing who and what it was.

Lord Wysely.

"Hell's fury," he barked, remembering that he was to have the sickness flags raised to ward off the man's arrival. It was too late now. Wysely and his entourage were close and would be here soon. Surina would not be pleased. He couldn't blame her. Wysely set Rawlin's teeth on edge as well. The spoiled, gluttonous sow had no redeeming qualities.

Rawlin donned a fresh tunic and finished dressing. He would find Surina and keep her close while Wysely was near. He did not trust the man, and knew while Wysely had not taken time to be trained properly in the arts of magik, he knew enough to be dangerous.

Chapter Five

Surina pushed open the wooden door to the healer's quarters as the afternoon light spilled in behind her, and looked around for signs of Yusoni, Head Healer to the House of Argyros. She saw no signs of the old man, nor did she hear his always-loud snores. He was probably in the kitchen sneaking treats—his favorite thing to do. That and spending time with the Helsena, the cook, whom she knew Yusoni had feelings for. Helsena had taken one look at Surina's hands and insisted she allow her to apply a salve Yusoni had left with her in the event the woman suffered a kitchen burn. The magical balm worked quickly. Already her hands were nearly back to normal, which was good, considering she didn't want to have to answer questions as to how she'd come by the burns.

Jaelyn knew of her lineage, as did her father and Yusoni. No others within the walls of the home were permitted such knowledge. Fear the information would one day fall into the wrong hands was too great. And her father took no risks with her life.

Jaelyn worked as a guard for her father and was a known Katarian. It was different for him. He had been granted a note of freedom when Surina was but a child, and had stayed on at the House of Argyros, working for her father. Though others knew what he was, they could not hold it against her father while he was a member of the senate. Should they learn he had wed an enemy and procreated with one, the end result being Surina, it would not go well for him. He would lose his backing from others and it would cost him his position and possibly his life.

A row of beds lined the right side of the large, rectangular room. The walls were painted a pale yellow, though she wasn't sure why. The yellow was not easy to wash blood from, evident by several stains upon the walls. Tightness took hold of her chest as she thought of the injuries she'd seen come through the healing quarters in her life. Men were sometimes hurt while training or if fights broke out in the slave quarters. And the arena games left many gravely wounded, some dead even.

Curtains, separating each bed, were drawn back on all except one on the far end. She hid her excitement, knowing Kritan was behind that curtain. She'd thought of him the entire time she'd bathed and dressed for dinner. From the moment she'd happened upon him with Dasin's men, Kritan had been all she could think about.

With soft steps, she covered the distance to the end of the room. If he was asleep, she didn't want to wake him. Though he surely required rest to properly heal, she couldn't stay away. She had to see him. She had to know he'd been tended to. That was only half the truth. If she were honest with herself, she wanted—*needed*—to see him again.

She pushed back the curtain, uncertain what she'd find. Kritan was there, asleep, his wounds having been tended and his body clean. He no longer wore her *palla*. It was clutched in his hand as he slept—much like how she'd clung to a blanket when she was but a child. The act was so innocent, so sweet that it was a sharp contradiction to the alpha she had both seen and sensed in him. It only served to make her like him more. He looked like a fallen, exhausted god.

For a long time she simply stood, studying him. Finally, she approached him and took a seat on the stool nearest his bed. Yusoni had a stool placed beside the bed so he or his apprentice could tend to the wounded with ease. A basin of water sat upon the table next to Kritan's bed. A washcloth was folded neatly near it. Surina wet the cloth and found herself running it over Kritan's knuckles to wash them. They were cracked, and while clean, still slightly bloody.

The lash marks on his torso and arms were covered in salve. Surina knew Yusoni's healing remedies were unmatched, but she didn't feel they were working fast enough. Kritan was a Katarian and their ability to self-heal was unparalleled, yet he had not healed fully yet. Guilt assailed her. He'd suffered at the hands of men employed by her father, though they had not been acting under her father's orders. As a female, she did not hold much authority outside the walls of her home, but within them, she was who spoke for her father.

Something inside her said Kritan deserved much better treatment than he'd received. And she was quite capable of giving as much.

She paused, her fingers caressing his. What was it about the man that made her sneak away to see him? Why did she feel so drawn to him? Was it because he was Katarian? Because he shared a link with her mother's people? She'd always been fascinated by them. By what she was half made up of. Maybe that had something to do with it. Though Kritan was hardly the first Katarian she'd ever met.

Jaelyn had been good about answering all her questions, even though he often seemed annoyed at the sheer number of them. Still, he did take the time to talk with her and even to teach her the Katarian language. She wished she'd paid more attention to the written Katarian word so that she would have been able to read Kritan's marks upon his arm.

Surina closed her eyes and drew upon her magik. While she wasn't the most powerful or trained with magiks, she had enough talent to hopefully help speed Kritan's healing process. She ran her hands over his knuckles and then up his arm. She kept going, kept pushing healing magiks through him as she kept her eyes closed, focusing on the task at hand. It was difficult to ignore how muscular he was. How hot and smooth his skin was. Her fingers skimmed the contour of each rippling muscle and her breathing quickened. Such an amazing build.

She rubbed his chest and then his torso. As she neared the top of the sheet covering his groin, something grabbed hold of her wrists. Her eyes snapped open. She gasped as she found Kritan holding her wrists gently, his dark gaze locked upon her.

"I'm sorry," she said in a hushed whisper. "I was only trying to heal you faster. I didn't mean to…"

He jerked her off the stool and with one yank had her on top of him. Her entire body thrummed with need. She should have screamed. Done something to alert the guards patrolling outside the quarters that he was awake and had her, but she didn't want the moment interrupted.

No.

She wanted him in all his feral glory. She shouldn't but she did.

He tightened his hold on her wrists and she whimpered. His expression softened. "You should not have been able to get that close to me while I slept. It is not something others can do."

She swallowed hard. "Sorry. Perhaps Yusoni gave you something to help you rest."

"Surina," he breathed out her name, his breath fanning over her lips.

She nearly melted on top of him out of sheer want. "Yes?"

His lips were suddenly on hers. Fire ignited within her and she lost all sense of reason as his tongue found hers. The kiss only lasted seconds but it burned into her memory. As he broke it, she nearly whimpered.

"Go," he snarled, even though he still had hold of her wrists, keeping her pulled tight to him.

She couldn't stop staring at his lips.

"Cease looking at me with such desire, woman, or I will fuck you."

Surina wasn't sure if that was a threat or a promise. She saw it as a bit of both. "I can't go. You're holding me to you."

He narrowed his gaze on her, his face becoming unreadable. "What magiks were you working on me? Spells of love and lust?"

A King's Ransom

He turned her hands to look at the palms. Healing him had healed the remainder of her burns as well. She found it strange that it should be so, but she had little time to ponder it.

"What?" She drew back as much as she could, her thigh grazing his clothed erection. "No. Healing spells."

"Says you," he replied, a look of skepticism on his face.

She tensed, realizing he might hurt her. There was something primal and raw in his gaze. A trickle of fear ran over her and she shivered on him.

He sniffed the air. "You are afraid of me now?"

She held perfectly still, unsure if she moved if it would provoke him more.

He sighed. "Surina, I would never harm you. Ever."

"But you think I tricked you? That I used lust magiks on you."

"I do not know what to—" He hissed and lifted her left arm, squeezing her wrist tight.

She cried out and he held their hands high, his gaze on his inner right arm. Surina forgot about the pain in the wrist as she watched a brand appearing on Kritan's skin. One and then another showed, followed by a third. She didn't understand what they said but he did. He tightened his hold on her more.

Tears welled. "K-Kritan, you're hurting me."

He released her wrists and sat her up, moving to a seated position with her in a matter of seconds. A testament to how strong he was. He lifted his right arm, staring harder at the marks, seeming bewildered at first before blinking and looking at her with wide eyes. He touched his inner arm where the new markings had appeared. The sheet, which already only just barely covered him, was pulled more by his movements.

"You? You are she?"

She rubbed her wrists as pain continued to shoot through them. She couldn't stop a tear from escaping.

Kritan wiped it from her cheek and then moved to touch her wrists again. She jerked her hands away and lowered her gaze.

"I'll go. I'm sorry I woke you," she said as she made an attempt to stand.

He caught hold of her gently and tugged her next to him. "Allow me to look at your wrists," he said, a softness to his voice.

She didn't protest as he lifted her hands and surveyed the angry red marks on her flesh. He sighed and shook his head, releasing her hands and standing. There was no sheet covering him.

She gulped.

He lowered his head. "The gods are wrong."

"The gods?" she asked, trying not to stare at his very naked, very close backside. The man was rock-hard muscle.

"Has your healer anything for your wrists?" he asked, refusing to make eye contact with her.

She couldn't stop looking at his ass. "What?"

He turned, his groin at eye level with her. "Surina."

She drew in a sharp breath. She'd never had such a clear look at a man's cock before. Without thought, she touched it lightly along the tip. Kritan grabbed his cock as it hardened, lengthening before her very eyes. He was huge—long, thick and clearly in want of her.

"Surina!"

She jolted. "Yes?"

"I wish you healed and you instead wish to tempt me? Already I fight the urge to fall upon you like a rutting beast. Is that what you want? Do you want me to ravish you?"

She thought upon it more and then met his gaze. "Yes."

He looked pained. "You are a lady. Demand better of me."

She pursed her lips, his cock still close enough to touch. It was close enough to put her mouth over and she did so hunger for it. "But I do want you. I can't explain why."

He lifted his arm, glancing at the newly formed markings. "I understand why."

She touched his upper thighs and licked her lips, her sights set on his cock. "Then explain it to me."

"Stop looking at me like that and stop touching me!"

Tipping her head to the side, she kept touching him, her hair falling over one shoulder. She moved her hands over his and touched his cock.

Kritan froze. "Surina, stop. I have only so much control."

"Am I hurting you?" she asked.

He shook his head. "But I fear I will hurt you."

Time seemed to slow as she thought upon her situation. She wanted to know the ways of things between a man and a woman, and she was drawn to Kritan in a way she'd never been drawn to another male before. This was her chance to know passion and she wouldn't miss out on it. She would not have an opportunity such as this again.

She released his cock and he seemed relieved right up until she then undid the knot holding up her tunic. It fell open to her waist, exposing her breasts to him. The cool air in the healer's quarters caused her nipples to harden at once. She almost covered her breasts with her arms, feeling too exposed, but she didn't. She sat with her head bent, fearing rejection.

Kritan moved over her with a speed she'd never seen anyone move with before. He pushed her back onto the bed and hiked up her tunic, his hands on her thighs as his mouth captured hers. She didn't protest. It was exactly what she wanted. His kisses were all she had imagined kisses could be and so very much more.

His hand eased between her legs and cupped the mound of her shaved pussy. Their tongues danced around one another erotically and she moaned into his mouth. He parted her slit and rubbed her clit, driving her mad with need. Pleasure tingled up her stomach and through her body with each flick of his finger over her clit.

Surina was helpless against his aggressive passions. Fear and anticipation filled her. His actions were so much more primitive, rough and raw than what she'd first imagined they'd be like. In that moment she knew however Kritan decided to fuck her, she'd let him.

Chapter Six

Kritan lay upon Surina, his mouth locked with hers as he started to dip a finger into her tight, wet channel. He met with resistance and withdrew his finger at once. She was untouched. The thought caused immense pride to swell within him, matched only by the guilt assailing him. The marks upon his arm stated clearly who she was to him.

His mate.

The marks told the story of them to date. They had met. They had shared desire for one another and they had begun forming a bond. One that could not be reversed.

He kissed her harder as he thought about his situation. He would not remain a captive long. He was sure of as much. As soon as he had his full strength, he would escape with ease. Leaving now wasn't an option, though. Not without Surina, and her home was here. He could not remain because he had responsibilities to his people and he would not live life as a slave. And even if he could talk her into joining him, which he doubted he could, she carried the blood of the Tamoni in her. His people would be hard to win over when trying to convince them she was their new queen.

Still, knowing the impossible situation he was in, Kritan could not stop kissing her, or touching her. As her hands fumbled along his upper arms and back, he sensed her stiffening under him. He drew back from their kiss and looked down upon her. She was deep in concentration. So much so it nearly made him laugh.

Her eyes were closed tight as she slid her hand over him at the most random of spots. "Step four," she whispered, placing a hand on his upper chest. "Step five."

He caught her wrist and her eyes snapped open. "Surina?"

She bit her lower lip. "Hmm?"

"What are you doing?"

"Waiting for you to have sex upon me," she answered.

Have sex upon her?

Her response did cause him to laugh, which he quickly covered with a cough. "I see. And the steps?"

She blushed. "Are from my scrolls. It's how I learned what to do. Why? Did I mess it up? I forgot a step, didn't I?" She bit her lower lip and touched his cheek. "One."

He smiled at her. "Surina."

"Two," she said, running her hand down his neck.

The hardness around his heart broke away as he looked down upon her sweet, innocent yet beautiful face. She was his, the gods had deemed it so and everyone else would simply have to learn to live with it. He could not leave her behind and his people would be told they must accept her, for she was his and already he knew he had feelings for her—feelings deeper than the raw lust finding one's true mate caused.

"Am I doing it wrong?" she asked, worry upon her brow. "You're laughing at me. Were the scrolls wrong? Were they incomplete?"

He kissed her forehead. "You are very special. Do you know that?"

She stared up at him. "Don't you want me anymore?"

"Oh, I want you. My cock is so hard it may never go down, but you deserve so much more than this. And I want our first joining to be something you remember fondly—that you look back upon knowing you were treated with respect. Not me rutting above you like a wild beast."

She continued to watch him, her hands skimming down his back, just above his ass.

"Surina, if I were to ask you to leave here with me, would you?"

She stiffened under him. "Leave my home?"

He dipped his head, sensing she needed to be kissed and persuaded. Kritan caught one of her wrists and guided her hand between them. He placed her hand upon his cock. She sucked in a deep breath.

"Kritan?"

"This pain," he said, rubbing her hand along the length of his erection, "is more than the guards could ever think to inflict. I ache for you. I want you so very much."

With a shy glance at his face, she nodded, her fingers caressing his cock on their own now. "I ache for you too."

Good. It was as it should be.

"Surina, you are naïve in the ways of a man and woman, and I will not have your first time be like this—with a slave in a healer's dwelling." He wanted to whisk her away to Katarius where he could lavish her in riches within the walls of his castle and lay her out on handspun silks to make love to her as a queen should be made love to.

She tugged at his cock. "I know you want more for me, but I want this. I want you. Please. Once my father returns I won't be allowed to sneak away to visit you like I want and…and I'm afraid if you are sent to the games, you won't return."

Lowering his head, he put his lips over one of her nipples. She squirmed under him, rotating her hips, her hands smashed between their bodies, still wrapped around his cock. He wanted to fuck her. It was all he wanted to do.

If he dared act upon his feral urges, he would cement the bond between them. He'd claim her fully and take her choices from her. She would not be able to stay among her people because she could not live without him—it was a hard truth for a mated pair. And he could not remain. A king of the enemy kingdom would not be welcome in

Tamonius. Should they discover his true identity, he would be bound to a cross in the center of Unus for all to see as he died a slow death.

And should he do as he wanted and bury himself deep within her, there was a better than average chance he would get her with child. While he had never entertained being a father before because the idea of finding his true mate seemed impossible, he had to admit the idea was intriguing. They were not ready for such things yet. Not while he was a captive. There was an order to things and this was not to be it, no matter how much he wanted it to be so.

"Surina, we…"

She opened her legs more and guided his cock to her entrance. The beast in him roared to the surface, confusing his sense of right and wrong. It wanted her and knew the man did as well. The animal could not understand what he was waiting for. Part of the man couldn't either.

She was there, willing and wanting.

"Kritan, please," she whispered as she kissed at his neck.

He somehow managed to hold back, just barely. Then she did the unthinkable, she bit his neck, and he lost his ability to reason at all. Raw need took hold of him and his body, and his mind and his beast came to an understanding. She was his and he would make sure of it.

He thrust into her, breaking through her virginal barrier. She cried out and he bent his head quickly, his mouth covering hers. He kissed her as he moved in and out of her. She wrapped her legs around his waist, making him go deeper into her tight, hot pussy. He had never known pleasure such as this. Had never known anything could feel this good.

She clawed at his upper arms, drawing fresh blood, confusing his senses more. Kritan could not stop himself as he pulled off her mouth, his incisors lengthening a moment before he bit her shoulder. His right arm burned and he knew that new marks were appearing. Ones stating he'd done the unthinkable. He'd fully claimed his mate.

Kritan pumped into her and she gasped, her pussy tightening around his cock even more, convulsing on it as she came. He pushed in and held there, releasing his seed, spurt after spurt. He let up on her shoulder and licked the wound. It healed over instantly before his eyes. Another sign she was his mate.

Surina stared up at him, her gaze full of passion. "You bit me."

"I did," he said, careful to keep his voice as soft as it could be in his current state. "Did I cause you pain?"

She tugged on his shoulders and he bent. She kissed him and then smiled against his lips. "Do it again."

He chuckled. His wife was demanding.

Wife.

The word sobered him. "Leave with me."

She stared up at him, looking lost as to how to respond.

"Surina!"

Kritan withdrew from her and stood quickly, facing her head guard. Rawlin was there in the entranceway to the healer's quarters, power whipping around him as he glared at Kritan's naked form. "Animal!"

"Rawlin, stop!" Surina screamed as she scrambled to get around Kritan.

Kritan caught her, keeping her behind him. He felt to be sure she was covered from Rawlin's view. She was. Thankfully she'd had the mindset to grab the sheet and use it to shield herself or Kritan might have let his hand shift forms before he lopped off the guard's head.

"Kritan, stop. He won't hurt me," she protested.

Rawlin curled his lip as he glared at Kritan. "You forced yourself upon her."

Surina gasped. "He did no such thing. I didn't give him a choice. I wanted him and wasn't going to take no for an answer."

71

Kritan lifted a brow. Should that story be relayed to his people, his head guards especially, he'd never live it down. He was the alpha, yet in a sense he had been tempted past the point of control by a mere virgin.

Rawlin shook with anger, his gaze going to Kritan's right arm. He focused on the band of marks that had not been there earlier. "Do those mean what I think they do?"

Kritan nodded.

Rawlin dropped his power and exhaled a shaky breath. "Surina. Come. Lord Wysely has arrived."

Surina touched Kritan's arm. "Wysely? But the sickness flags?"

"Were not put out," Rawlin snapped. "Come. You must be presentable for him. Now you look like a used woman."

Kritan grabbed Rawlin by the throat, his beast nearing the surface. He growled.

Surina pushed between the men. "Kritan, no. Stop. He's angry with me. Don't hurt him. Please."

Rawlin's gaze was challenging, but Kritan released him because Surina asked it of him. He turned his attention to Surina and touched her cheek, unconcerned with the fact he was still naked. "Go and greet your visitor, my flower. I will be here when you are done. We have much to discuss."

Chapter Seven

Surina leaned, propped up on her arm on the mass of pillows and linens, one grouping of many surrounding the fountain in the center of the dining hall. The room was set up to be inviting and relaxing. The walls, painted a deep purple, gave a rich feeling to the room. Too bad the room was filled with Lord Wysely and his companions. No amount of paint or fine linens could make up for the foulness of Wysely and his entourage.

Her stomach churned as Lord Wysely lounged on his side, partially on an orange pillow with gold fringe, biting large chunks of meat from the bone he held—his fourth leg of *halunaian* beast in a matter of thirty minutes. As he chewed, he laughed, causing flecks of food to spray in all directions. He seemed unconcerned with the image he presented.

The pillow would need to be burned. There was no way she was keeping it and using it again. Not with the stench of Wysely's sweat upon it, as well as most of his dinner.

His beady eyes glanced again in her direction and she pressed a smile to her face despite the bile rising in her throat. Gazlonia, a kitchen maid, approached with a pitcher of wine and topped off Surina's cup. Gazlonia glanced in Wysely's direction and lifted a brow, her gaze returning to Surina.

Surina hid her laughter and winked. She had known Gazlonia all her life and already knew what the woman was thinking, for Surina was thinking it as well. She hoped Wysely would choke on a bone.

Gazlonia hurried away, the gold chains on her wrists and ankles rattling as she did. Surina wished she could run as well. Sadly, she was trapped, forced by protocol to entertain her house guest in her father's absence.

May the gods curse Rawlin for forgetting to put up the sickness flags.

Had he set out the flags, Wysely would have turned and fled. Now Wysely and his entourage—a small group of guards, three male servants and three female servants—all remained close, each looking as devious as the next. She truly hoped Rawlin would wake with a case of childhood spots come morning and that they would be centered upon his groin.

That would teach him.

She didn't want to be at a dinner for an *honored* guest. She wanted to be with Kritan. Rawlin had basically shoved her into the dining hall and stormed off, refusing to make eye contact with her since finding her naked and beneath Kritan. She wanted to believe Rawlin wouldn't order Kritan harmed—that Rawlin would know doing such a thing would forever make her hate him. Still, she worried. She'd never seen Rawlin so angry before and so hurt.

He had always been sworn to duty and to protect. She thought him incapable of certain emotions, like extreme anger directed at her. Apparently, she'd been wrong. He could be angered to the point he could not stand to look upon her.

He'd tell her father of her indiscretion. She groaned, a wave of apprehension coming over her as she thought more upon Kritan's question—if she'd leave with him. Perhaps she should. It could make everything better. She wouldn't have to suffer her father's disappointment and wrath. She'd be away from Rawlin and his anger. It could be for the best. But could she do such a thing? Leave her childhood home, her father, her friends, her family?

Stop thinking as a child would. Take a stand. Demand what you want.

Rawlin needed to realize she was a grown woman with a grown woman's needs. She didn't walk about the estate playing with dolls and asking to braid the guards' hair. She hadn't done that in nearly fifteen summers. She was a woman now. There was no point in denying it, and if she hadn't been before Kritan, she certainly was now. He'd seen to that.

Her body ached for his touch. She eyed the archway, wondering when she could sneak away to find him again. He had said they needed to speak. She agreed and she wanted to be near him, wanted to be held by him. Strange, all that had happened in such a short span of time. A testament to the gods and destiny being at play. Though, should her father speak of such things, of gods and destiny, he would not be pleased.

Needing to channel her energy, she focused upon the vintage fountain in the center of the room. It was from long ago, when the planet's inhabitants still traveled the stars and had used technologies that were now forbidden. Her father had the fountain's electronic components removed, knowing the backlash of owning a piece in working order was severe. She wished she'd been able to see it when it did far more than simply toss water into the air. Her father told her that at one point in his life, the fountain had been used as a seer's tool, allowing the viewer to commune with other planets.

She could only imagine what life must have been like then. So much to see. So much to do. Not that her father would have permitted her to do or see any of it. Inter-planetary travel had been a way of life. Whatever had happened, no other planet dared to attempt to visit Panucia. It was as if the galaxies feared them.

She let her magik up and out, allowing it to run over the fountain. While she was nowhere near powerful enough to commune with another kingdom, let alone another planet, she was powerful enough to do parlor tricks. The water changed from clear to a bright, vibrant pink. Everyone clapped and continued with their food and drink.

Dasin and his guard friends entered the dining hall and Surina tensed. Wysely didn't need any encouragement on how to be a bigger sow. He was quite good all on his own. Surina sat up partially, wondering what was keeping Rawlin from returning. It wasn't like him to leave her totally unattended when a guest was present. Especially when the guest was Wysely. Though guest was such a nice word. Parasite on the ass of the people was more appropriate.

Why he'd come at all when he'd known her father to be away was a mystery to her. If he thought for one moment she'd entertain his all-too-frequent advances, he was mistaken. She would never be satisfied by a man such as him, even if she hadn't experienced a man like Kritan.

Powerful.

Alpha.

Her body tingled at the mere thought of him. It was only by chance she noticed Dasin moving closer to the women in Wysely's group. As one of the women slinked her hands up and under Dasin's tunic, clearly stroking his cock, Surina stiffened. Her father would not have stood for this type of behavior within the walls of his estate. Not with Surina home.

Cursed Theanius, Rawlin, where are you?

Dasin moved closer to Wysely. "Tell me you have brought them to share with us."

"Even better," Wysely said, sitting up, a piece of half-chewed meat stuck to one of his chins. Grease coated his lips and his fingers. He motioned to the women with him. "Put on our show. Let them see what we prepared." He looked to Surina. "You will love it."

Doubtful.

She did her best to appear genial when all she wanted to do was retch and then run from him and his companions. She fidgeted with the thin, red material of her *palla* draped over her body. Unlike other women, Surina wore an additional layer beneath the *palla* and tunic, having no desire to gift Wysely any glimpses of her body.

Wysely's women began petting and undressing each other, their tongues lacing. The males he'd brought with him joined in and Surina shifted uncomfortably. She didn't want to be stuck in the room while they had an orgy.

The only sex she wanted to be witness to was what would happen between her and Kritan. No more. And she especially did not want to see Lord Wysely naked.

She nearly passed out from the thought of such a horrific event occurring.

Dasin and his guards clapped as the three male slaves began to slap around the females. Surina sat up more, on alert. The women smiled, fire in their eyes as they shoved themselves at the males, as if they wanted to be hit again. The men did so. This was not erotic. It was sickening.

She looked away, the nauseating thuds sounding all around her. There was a gasp and then one of the women cried out. Surina glanced at her to find she had a cock rammed in her ass. The male behind her pumped with a fury as another man slapped at the woman's breasts. Dasin's men moved in and Wysely nodded, waving his hand and giving them permission to join in the fun.

They did.

Dasin remained on the sidelines, his gaze sweeping to her as if he wanted to gauge her reaction to such violent acts of sex. Now that Dasin's guards had joined in, it was sheer chaos. Surina ripped her attention from him and found the only other place to put it was on the show.

Wysely sat up more, clapping, elation in his eyes as one of the guards wrapped a tunic around a woman's wrists, holding them as another of the guards lined up with her entrance. The woman seemed eager to be fucked by many men at once while bound. She wiggled and flashed a smile. "Fuck me hard or not at all."

The guard did as instructed. It looked brutal to Surina.

One of the guards grabbed the woman's mouth and tugged it open. He poured wine straight from a pitcher down the woman's throat, making her choke, and then slapped her face, laughing as she sputtered and spit. She looked wild for a moment and then excited.

"Do it again," she demanded. "This time with your cum."

Surina closed her eyes. Etiquette be dammed, she didn't want to see anymore.

Dasin was suddenly next to her, his hand on her cheek. "My dearest Surina. Is this too much for your virginal eyes to behold?"

She wasn't a virgin anymore but she held that bit to herself. Instead, she stiffened. He lowered himself, putting his body near hers in her semi-lounging position. She felt like a trapped animal. She tried to pull away.

"I would not if I were you," he warned. "Rawlin is in a mood and has left the main house. That means you are alone here since your other guards are on a fool's errand—one I sent them on. Should you pull away from me now, I will tell Lord Wysely you wish to partake in the show."

"You would not dare," she whispered, unable to believe Rawlin would leave her without one of her other guards near. Something was wrong. Dasin was never quite this bold with her.

"I would. And then all would hear of how you gave yourself to him and his people. You would be ruined and forced into a marriage with him." Dasin caught her chin and forced her to look upon Wysely as he lifted his tunic and grabbed hold of his pathetic cock. He began stroking it, watching the show, watching as his slaves were fucked by Dasin's guards.

She recoiled at the idea of the man touching her.

Dasin laughed in her ear, pressing himself tighter against her, his covered erection digging at her backside. "Then we agree. You pick me over him."

If she screamed or tried to bring attention to the situation, there was a better than average chance no one who could help would hear. If the servants came to aid her, Dasin would find a way to hurt them. And gods forbid if Rawlin returned in his current state.

She shuddered.

He was so angry with her she wasn't sure what he'd do. She'd like to think he'd help her, but she wasn't so sure after the way he'd behaved towards her.

Lucila entered the dining hall and nearly dropped the tray she was holding when she spotted Dasin near Surina. With a quick shake of her head Surina tried to warn her friend away. It was too late. One of Wysely's guards caught hold of Lucila.

"What do we have here?" he asked. "I want her."

"She is not for the taking," Surina said, trying to sit up, only to be held in place by Dasin.

"Isn't she?" he asked, his lips pressed to her ear. "She has fucked nearly all the men who reside within the house. Me included. She likes sex, Surina. My men tell me she sucked Rawlin's cock just last night before allowing him to ram into her pussy."

From the expression of fear on Lucila's face, she did not like the idea of being involved in this. Surina couldn't blame her.

"No," Surina said. "She is not to be part of this *show*."

"Release her," Dasin said to Wysely's guard. "Leave."

Lucila remained in place, her gaze on Surina. "Mistress?"

Dasin snarled. "If you stay, you agree to be fucked, am I clear? My men will not be kind. They will not make you come. They will be brutal. They will fuck you until you bleed."

Lucila shook but she didn't leave. Surina knew why. Lucila was scared to leave Surina alone. With tear-filled eyes, Surina looked to her friend. "Go. Please."

"I will not," Lucila said.

"Then she has made her choice." Dasin snapped his fingers. Two of his men went for Lucila.

Surina screamed and twisted in Dasin's arms, trying to get free. "Stop. No."

"What will you do to keep her safe?" he asked.

She sighed. "Anything."

Dasin twisted her face, bringing his lips to hers. His breath was hot as he kissed her, forcing his tongue into her mouth. She didn't fight him but she didn't make it easy for him either. He grinned and pulled back, his eyes burning mad with lust.

"I say we see how tight the serving whore's cunt is," Wysely added. "I do so like my women blonde, and I want to see her fucked until she bleeds. Come suck me and then I will be the judge of your cunt."

Surina yanked at Dasin. "You have the power to stop this. I beg of you, do so."

Wysely practically jumped up and down in one spot with glee, one hand on his cock. "Come. Suck me!"

Surina's stomach revolted wildly.

Dasin touched her neck gently. "You are mistaken. *You* have the power to end this." He leaned in. "Agree to lie with me and I shall see to it this fat sow is gone and that your friend, the handmaiden, is unharmed."

To give herself to a man she hated? Could she? It would not be like lying with Kritan. Nothing would ever be like that. She knew as much.

As one of the warriors began to lift his tunic, his gaze on Lucila, she had her answer. She looked to Dasin and teared up. "Yes. Stop this now."

A large, sinister smile broke over Dasin's face. "Cease. You, sir," he said, looking towards Wysely. "It would appear your time here has ended."

"What?" Wysely asked, staring at Lucila. "I want to fuck this one. I want to watch her bleed."

"Another time perhaps," Dasin said. "For now, it is time to retire for the evening."

Wysely continued to protest but it fell upon deaf ears. Dasin had his guards escort Wysely and his entourage to their quarters and surprised Surina by instructing his men to see Lucila safely to her chambers.

When they were alone, Surina tensed, expecting Dasin to force himself upon her.

He put his hand out to her and helped her to her feet. "Come, Surina. We shall not do this here, like animals. We shall go to my chambers. I want to see you spread out upon my bed. I want your scent to cover my sheets."

She gulped and nodded. As she pressed her hand to his, she had to fight from being sick. He led her from the dining hall and out into the courtyard. The guard's housing complex was close, yet Dasin walked her past it. She shuffled her feet as they approached the healer's

81

quarters. Her thoughts went instantly to Kritan. She didn't want to see him hurt because of her.

"Dasin," she said softly. "Where is it we go?"

He pulled her closer to him. "I have thought more upon it. There is a chance we will be interrupted if we are within my quarters, and I will spend the entire night within you, Surina. I want for nothing to disturb us."

She gasped and tugged to get her hand back.

He looked down at her. "Are you backing out now? Do you wish for me to have your friend retrieved? I will have six of my men fuck her at once. They will take turns with her until she is broken beyond repair."

"Why are you this way?" she asked. "You are not an ugly man, yet your actions say otherwise."

He met her gaze, seeming confused.

"When I first met you, I found you to be most handsome a man."

"More so than Rawlin?" he asked.

Women whispered often when Rawlin was near, each wondering how and when they might be able to bed him. Surina knew Rawlin was considered most pleasing to the eye and sought after by others. "I found you very pleasing to look upon," she said, unable to tell him he was better looking than Rawlin.

Dasin raked his gaze over her. "Then why refuse me?"

"Your actions," she stated evenly. "You are cruel. You gain much pleasure from others' suffering and that, to me, stains you. It takes your gifted outside appearance and rots it before my very eyes."

"You are saying if I were more like your dear, sweet Rawlin, you would still see me as most pleasing to look upon?"

She wasn't sure what his obsession with Rawlin was. "I guess. Yes."

Dasin's nostrils flared. "I am not soft like he is. I do not bend to your every whim. I find you to be spoiled and a woman who knows not her place." He pushed her backwards and into the wall of the healer's quarters. "Your father shields you from life and the way of it. You are naïve and should learn to obey the men around you. Especially since your dear father will not be returning. There is a surprise waiting for him in Unus."

She struggled against him. "Dasin, stop. Please."

"You told me I could lie with you if I released the female." A sick smile came over him. "You should know she is being used by my guards as we speak. She is a whore. And your father probably begs for life as they nail him to a cross—the traitor!"

Surina gasped. "I hate you!"

"I know," he said with a smile. "It matters not to me. Rawlin is off having a temper tantrum. No one will come to assist you, Surina. You are at my mercy. I suggest you get used to begging. It is what you will spend the night doing. And when your father does not return, do not think my men and I cannot handle Rawlin. We will end him and then you will be mine to do with as I please—for good."

He thrust a hand up and under her tunics.

She was no match for him physically, but magikally she was a threat indeed. She let her power rise. He laughed. "Do it. I dare you. If you do, I will order your cunt of a friend to be killed. Do you wish for her death upon your hands?"

"N-no," she answered.

"Then I suggest you try to enjoy yourself," he said. "I know I will."

Tears flowed freely and she closed her eyes tight. She wouldn't let Lucila be killed. She'd do what had to be done. Dasin's finger found her slit. He parted it and a second before he would have thrust a finger into her, he was ripped free of her.

Sucking in a huge breath, Surina opened her eyes to find Kritan there. He twisted, striking Dasin and then crouching, preparing himself for battle as Dasin recovered from the blow. Dasin charged him, hate burning in his eyes. Kritan seemed in control yet over the edge, all at once. He ducked and then came up, turning and kicking Dasin before spinning and knocking him high into the air. Surina watched, unable to believe it was all happening. Dasin's limp body was to the side. He was alive, barely.

Kritan's chest heaved as he spun and stared at her, looking feral and lethal. "Are you harmed?"

She could barely think.

His dark gaze swept over her. "Are *you* harmed?"

"No," she squeaked.

He turned to go at Dasin again. Claws emerged from his fingertips as fur sprouted up his arm.

Surina covered her mouth, her eyes wide. She had seen Jaelyn shift forms before but never with the intent to do harm. She shook her head. She didn't want to witness this. "Don't. As a slave, the others will kill you for taking his life. I will not have your death be because you were protecting me."

Kritan stopped a second before he'd have ended Dasin. His gaze moved to her. He looked from her to his hand and then took a few moments before retracting his claws. He seemed almost ashamed— afraid to gaze at her.

Unable to help herself, she rushed to him and tossed her arms around his neck. He wrapped his arms around her and lifted her off her feet. She buried her face in his neck and savored his manly smell. She sobbed openly, whispering again and again how thankful to him she was.

He held her close, rocking her body. "Shh, my flower, I have you. None will harm you."

Chapter Eight

Kritan held his mate to him. She was soft, supple against his hard frame as if she'd been made to fit him. Fear continued to pulse from her and he hated that he'd nearly not made it in time to help her. While he had sensed her approaching the healer's quarters long before she reached them, he'd been thinking of a way to leave with her. He had only just settled on the idea of abducting her and letting all in Tamonius think he'd taken her for ransom when he'd caught her scent riding the night air. It was her fear that radiated to him and pulled him to his senses and from his cunning plan to steal away with her in the night.

It was a perfectly reasonable idea. He'd take her and not look back. Should any come to seek her, he'd start a war to keep her.

Seemed simple enough to him.

He paused in reflection, realizing logic had escaped him and fallen by the wayside to the needs of his heart.

When he'd heard Surina's soft voice shaking with fear and then heard the guard, Dasin, threatening her, he'd instantly wanted to shift forms and kill the man. He was still weakened from his time being held captive, but he was much stronger than he had been at their last encounter. Surina had seen to that when she'd gifted him her healing through her magiks.

When he'd caught sight of the guard trying to defile her, he'd snapped, losing hold of his hard fought self-control. The beast had gripped him and wanted a pound of flesh as payment for harming his woman.

Mine.

He kissed the top of her head as she trembled in his arms. He hated that he'd not acted sooner, taking her away from Tamonius and straight back to Katarius with him.

"All is well now, Surina."

"When he wakes, he will have you killed," she sobbed, her haunted gaze going to Dasin's body. "My father isn't here to stop him and Rawlin's anger with me is unlike anything I have seen before. He will not stop Dasin."

The guard could try. Kritan would welcome the challenge. He wanted to kill the man and looked forward to the opportunity.

Surina skimmed her lips over his collarbone. "Thank you," she whispered. "I know not what I'd have done if you had not arrived."

"Allow me to kill him," he said, unsure why he sought her permission.

Because she is your mate, you dolt.

She kissed higher upon his neck, shaking in his arms. His cock responded but he knew now was not the time. She had nearly been taken against her will. He would not seek pleasures of the flesh from her now. "Allow me to see you to the main house."

"You want me gone so you can kill him," she said, still crying.

She was right. He had every intention of ending the guard's life. Dasin had dared to harm his mate. That was an act punishable by death within his kingdom and by his kind. It mattered not he was no longer upon his own soil. The man had crossed a line, one he would not be permitted to cross again.

He sighed, knowing a lie was the best course of action. Sadly, in his experience, women could not always handle hard truths and often required to be told what they needed to hear. "Of course not. Come. The healer is out cold, having drunk too much of his own special brew. Rest with me on this night as we plan our escape."

She stiffened. "I can't go with you. I can't leave my father."

Kritan scented her head guard. Rawlin was frantic, fear racing through him as he hunted for her. A low growl emanated from the back of Kritan's throat. Rawlin had left her unguarded with Dasin.

Unacceptable.

"Surina?" Rawlin called out.

Surina pressed herself to Kritan harder as if she wanted to climb through him. He held her close, his cock still aching to be within her again.

Rawlin burst through the path, his sword already drawn. His gaze widened as he spotted Dasin's limp body. With a shaky hand, Rawlin returned his sword to its ring upon his waist. "Did he do as he wished with her?"

"No," Kritan said. "No thanks to you. Why was she unguarded? You are head guard to her, yet this is the second time she has been alone with this, this…" His beast tried to surface. His mouth burned with the change, his teeth lengthening at an alarming rate. He tried to step back from Surina but she yelped, clinging to him more.

She looked up at him and he waited for the fear to come. None did. She went to her tiptoes, cupped his face and then put her forehead to his mouth.

"From the bottom of my heart, I thank you," she said. "I had no wish for what we shared on this day to be soiled by him. For him to enter me would have—" She began to cry again and he gained control of his beast.

He disliked seeing a woman cry. Always had. He didn't know too many men who did not wince at the sight of such a thing. Hardened warriors had been brought to their knees by the tears of women for centuries.

Kritan tilted her chin up and kissed her tenderly. "My flower, no tears or I will be forced to kill the guard. Already I teeter on the edge. Your tears make me want to kill things." He glared over her head at Rawlin. "Why was she unguarded? Again?"

Rawlin looked away, shame in his gaze. Kritan surmised his answer. He snorted. "Your jealousy left my mate at the mercy of an evil man."

"Mate?" Surina questioned.

"Shh," he said, too focused on Rawlin to want to stop and explain the way of things to her. It was not as if she had any say in the matter now, after the fact. She would be told soon enough that she was wife to him and she would have to accept as much.

He continued to hold Rawlin with his steely gaze. "He wished to have his way with her, and from what I overhead, believes her father dead and her place by his side. What do you know of this?"

Surina drew back somewhat. "He lies."

She gasped as if only just recalling something of importance.

"Lucila!"

Rawlin lifted a hand. "Is safe and well. I happened upon Lucila and Dasin's men inside the main house. I saw to her safety personally. She rests now in the chamber next to yours. It is where I thought you might want her to be. And men loyal to me now watch over her."

Surina turned slightly, keeping her body to Kritan's. He wrapped an arm around her. He liked her close.

"Rawlin, Dasin said Father will not return from Unus. That a surprise waited for him there."

The expression on Rawlin's face said he'd suspected as much. He cleared his throat. "I have sent a runner to check on the status of your father. I dispatched him two days prior. He should return by morning with word."

89

"Do you think Dasin spoke truth?" she questioned the guard before looking to Kritan. "Do you think my father is dead?"

Kritan hated seeing his mate in pain. He touched her cheek tenderly. "I know naught of your father, but if he is anything like you—stubborn and resourceful—I suspect he is safe and well."

Rawlin shook his head and Kritan knew then the runner fable had been created to put Surina at ease, at least for a short period. Kritan kissed her lips again. "My flower, go within the healer's quarters and await me there. I must speak with your guard."

She nodded and did as she was instructed to do. Once she was safely inside, Kritan faced Rawlin. The time had come for the two of them to have words, whether the guard wanted to or not. "Tell me all of what you know. I cannot keep her safe if you shroud truths with lies."

Rawlin walked to Dasin and knelt, touching his neck. "He lives?"

"She did not wish for me to kill him," Kritan said, shaking his head. "The woman has no sense. He will make an attempt on her again if I do not."

Rawlin met his gaze. "Who are you, really? You're no mere gladiator."

Kritan entertained continuing his charade, but realized his own rules must apply to him as well if Surina was to remain safe. "Kritan of Katarius, born to the House of Lanacious, first son to Ionius, leader of the Katarian army and…"

Rawlin gasped. "King to Katarius."

An incline of his head was all Kritan offered.

Rawlin stood slowly.

"Know this, Magik," Kritan warned, his gaze steady, his body ready to fight should the need arise. "I have completed the bonding ritual with Surina. She is my mate and my wife. This is not something a Katarian can undo, and once mated, one cannot live without the other.

To betray me is to betray her. While I know the fires of jealousy burn deep within you, I know also you hold love for her, that you would not wish her harm."

Rawlin's shoulders slumped, defeat evident. "Yet that is precisely what I brought upon her on this night. I left her with Lord Wysely. I was hurt, and in my rage I punished her by leaving her with him—which gave Dasin the opportunity he has been seeking to be alone with her. Then word reached me of an attack upon Argyros's caravan and my thoughts went to him, not Surina—she was alone with them." He closed his eyes. "I did this."

Kritan wanted to punish him, but it was clear he was doing a fine job on his own, without Kritan's assistance. "Make it right, Magik."

A knowing look came over Rawlin as he lifted his hand. Magik sprang forth from him and went directly at Dasin's limp form. Dasin's head twisted all the way around, cracking loudly. There was no mistaking the sound of death.

"She cannot be permitted to find his body," Kritan said, crossing his arms over his chest, impressed with the man's power but not so much so he was willing to admit to as much. "In her state she will not take it well."

Rawlin waved his hand and Dasin's body burned to ash instantly. Kritan held his gasp of surprise, just barely. He had heard tales of ones who could do such a thing. They were High Magik Legionnaire Knights of the First Order from the Valley of the Dead and thought long gone.

Clearly, like the Fornication Hags, rumors of their demise were exaggerated.

He was sensing a theme.

"His men?" Kritan asked.

"Have been dealt with already," Rawlin responded calmly as if he had not just made a body burn away to nothingness with but a wave of his hand. "They are no longer a threat and broke quickly in giving away the names of others behind this act against Argyros. Those responsible have launched their plans into action. They will seek out Surina next to make an example of her before all of Tamonius."

"Like hell!" Kritan snapped. He knew all too well what happened to those the Tamoni wanted to make examples of. It was not kind.

"I can get you out of Tamonius," Rawlin said, nearing him. "But before I do, you must know something."

Kritan looked him up and down, wondering what else the magik had up his sleeve to share. "That you are in love with my wife? I am aware of as much."

"That but something more," he said. "Something you will find troubling to hear."

Kritan continued to watch him.

"Argyros was not alone on his journey to Unus. He took with him a group of four guards, one of which was his most trusted advisor and a friend to me." He exhaled slowly. "Learning the truth of who you are explains much, mostly why you would end up here, of all places. Jaelyn, your brother, was a good man and a great soldier. He was a loyal friend to Argyros and held great love for Surina—seeing her as family and teaching her much of the ways of your people."

Kritan swayed as the meaning of Rawlin's words sank into him. Jaelyn was part of the House of Argyros and now he was dead? He maintained an even façade. "Tell me what the runner said."

"He only knew that Argyros, Jaelyn and the others were ambushed just outside the walls of Unus. There was too much blood and body parts to sort out who was who, but that none survived."

Kritan pulled upon his years of conditioning and his leadership skills, refusing to lose himself in grief. Not now. Not when his mate needed him most. "These enemies of Argyros—they will come here first?"

"Yes. They will be close. If we can get Surina from here, there is a chance they will not slaughter all who dwell here, but rather continue to hunt for her, in the wrong direction, I hope." He squared his shoulders. "She will not want to go. She will want to stay in hopes she can protect those who dwell within. My men will stay and try to protect those who remain."

"Freeing them is not an option?" Kritan asked.

Rawlin huffed. "They are marked, known slaves. To send them out into the streets of Tamonius unguarded and without a master is to send them to their deaths. At least here they have a fighting chance."

"Yet the chance is not so great Surina can remain?" he asked, already knowing the answer.

"They will stop at nothing to have her. She is daughter to a powerful man—a martyr now. She must be made an example of by them or their cause dies as quickly as it began."

"Then we should leave now," Kritan said.

"I agree. I will secure a wagon or some mode of transportation. You must convince her to leave with us."

"Set them free," Surina said from the doorway of the healer's quarters. "Set the servants free. Let them have a chance. They could survive, you do not know for sure they will not. Tell them they can either go or stay."

Kritan stared at his mate, surprised by her courage and strength.

"See to that and I will go with you both," she said, hugging herself. She took a deep breath. "I am sorry for the loss of your brother. I too loved him."

"Surina," he said.

She held a hand up. "I will wake Yusoni. He should leave as well despite the fact he is a freeborn."

She headed into the healer's quarters.

Rawlin did not move. "We must make a stop in Vesta and then we will go on through Unus and to the ports. We will have to use caution, but it is the quickest way to find passage to Katarius."

The idea of entering Vesta again held little appeal to him. "What is in Vesta?"

"Power," Rawlin returned. "And we are in need of it if we are to try to help the House of Argyros. Mark my words, King, your wife will not truly leave if she believes anyone here is unprotected and the slaves will not choose freedom. They have made a home here. They will defend it."

Chapter Nine

Kritan sat in the back of the wagon, reclining against the backboard as he held Surina to him. At the front, Rawlin handled the lead to the horses, steering the wagon over the bumpy terrain. First light wasn't far off as they'd traveled through the night from the country estate. Rawlin assured him that Vesta was near. Reservations still plagued Kritan about returning to the city he'd been ambushed in. Rawlin swore the power they required to help protect the House of Argyros could be found there. Kritan wasn't a believer. Beyond filth, depravity and violence, Vesta offered little.

His free hand went to the sword and shield Rawlin had given him prior to their departure. His own were tucked away safely at the ports where he'd paid good money to someone he trusted to ensure they would be there when he returned—however long that would take.

No longer was Kritan dressed as a slave. Now he looked as though he were a guard from Tamonius, wearing a white tunic, a red cloak, a gold snake brooch and a gold-colored, roped tie at his waist. It would do to see Surina to safety and then he would burn the garments.

He kissed his mate's temple as she continued to rest as best she could. She had been brave as Rawlin announced the fall of her father to the household. Even braver still when she'd stepped forth to tell the slaves they could have freedom or remain within the walls of the house and take a stand with the guards. Kritan was surprised to see that no slaves left. They made a stand together, looking at one another and nodding as if all were in agreement.

They would be united against the enemies of Argyros.

A handmaiden named Lucila had helped to pack a light bag for Surina and had hugged his wife tightly before they'd departed. He knew the two were close and knew Surina worried about the woman's well-being.

Her sleep was fitful at best.

Rawlin glanced at him. "How is she?"

He shook his head, drawing Surina against him more. She turned slightly and lay partway on him, her knee moving towards his groin. Her palm came to a rest on his chest and he breathed in her flowery scent. He knew exhaustion held her in its grip and that sadness for the loss of her father was upon her. He understood her loss. He felt it too.

He'd been so close to finding Jaelyn. Close to making amends. But it would never be.

He kissed Surina's head. She stirred awake and stared up at him with sleepy eyes. "Shh, rest. We will stop soon enough and you need your sleep," he said softly.

She ran a hand over his scruffy jawline. "I need you."

Kritan glanced at Rawlin and noted the man's stiff posture. He knew Rawlin could hear what was said between him and Surina. "My flower, sleep."

"Kritan," she said, her hand skimming down his chest and settling on his cock. "Please. I need you. Make me forget all that has happened, all that I have learned on this night."

"Surina." He caught her wrist gently. "Now is not the time."

Her lips moved over his, silencing his protest. The smell of her wanting cunt made his cock harden. She wanted him and he her, but not with Rawlin close. He would not share the moment with a man who desired her flesh. As she slipped her hand up and under his tunic, going straight to his erection, Kritan stiffened. Her kisses came faster.

She pumped his cock and eased herself over him more. Had he not known she'd been a virgin before being with him, he'd have thought her an experienced lover in that moment, for she did not hesitate as she moved her tunic up and slipped her wet cunt onto his cock. It encased him tightly, reminding him of how good she felt. She moved on him, riding him slowly at first, her tongue lacing with his, their bodies joined. She increased her pace and Kritan seized hold of her hips, controlling her movements, wanting to prolong their pleasure.

He controlled her hips just so, creating a figure-eight pattern with her movements. Her cunt pulled at his cock as if demanding his seed. Kritan thrust up, unable to stand the slow, sweet torture anymore. He had to have her fully. He had to possess her, witnesses be damned. White-hot waves of enjoyment crashed over him as he fucked her with feral need. Animal noises came from him but he didn't care.

Surina panted on him, her body pliable, as if she knew he had to take what he needed now. In the end their wants were the same. He moved, grinding her against him, knowing he was giving her additional stimulation that she required as he continued to bury himself balls-deep in her cunt.

When her pussy fluttered around his shaft, he growled in masculine triumph. His balls tightened a second before he found release. Surina's lips greeted his and she bit at his mouth, her pussy continuing to pulse on him, a sign of her finding pleasure as well.

Surina slid her hands lower, finding his on her hips. She intertwined her fingers with his and stayed on him as they kissed. The more Kritan thought upon it all, the more he realized he'd permitted a near-virgin to do as she pleased with him and gain her way.

He smiled against her lips.

His wife had him wrapped around her little fingers. There was no denying it.

As he drew in a deep breath, he caught scent of Rawlin's arousal. Kritan tensed and withdrew from his mate. The action did not go without the telltale sound of a cock leaving a wet, tight pussy.

Surina eased next to him and pushed her tunic down, covering her backside and most of her legs once more. Kritan adjusted himself, his gaze going to the front of the wagon then to Rawlin who sat rigid. His desire rolled off him so much so that it would have knocked Kritan over had he been standing.

"Thank you," Surina said, kissing his cheek.

"Anytime, my flower."

Rawlin chanced a glance back at Kritan. Kritan sat up, staring intensely at the guard. "Yes?"

"We are here," Rawlin stated.

Surina touched Kritan's chest and it was then she realized what she'd done with him had been overheard by Rawlin. Her cheeks flamed pink and she hid her face against his arm.

"He has been around a long time, my flower," Kritan said. "He has overheard a couple pleasing one another before. And I do not think him a virgin. Do you?"

"No."

"Then worry not on it. Come. We have arrived," he said, helping her up and out of the wagon. He grabbed the sword Rawlin had given him and slid it through the ring on the waist cord of his tunic. As Kritan took in his surroundings, he growled, extending claws from one hand. "What trickery is this?"

They stood outside the very tavern he'd been ambushed in. The very one guards of magik lines had waited in, staging a ruse to confuse his senses before attacking him with a fury. The same guards who had then tortured him for information on the Katarian army.

The ones he'd refused to tell anything to despite their torture, despite their abuse. He was a king. Not some sniveling weakling who cowed in fear at the first sight of danger. He had not given them any information.

Rawlin appeared confused. He arched a brow as he tied off the horses. "What is your problem now?"

"You," Kritan said, glancing to the tavern. "You pretend to be so different from the others yet you are the one in charge. You are the one behind it all. The puppet master."

"What in bloody hell do you speak of?"

"This is where I was taken from after being ambushed," Kritan said, growling.

Rawlin rolled his eyes, unimpressed. "I had nothing to do with you being taken, fool. Control your animal or I will control it for you."

"Do not threaten me," Kritan snarled, anger bristling through him. He was ready and willing to tear the man to bits, and he suspected it had more to do with Rawlin's attraction to his mate and less to do with thinking he might have betrayed him. Jealousy was something Katarian males struggled with once they found their mates. He'd heard tales told of it, but had not believed them to be true. He had never thought he'd want to kill first and ask questions later when it came to a woman. Oh, how wrong he'd been. Right now he wanted nothing more than to end Rawlin. Since he could not because it would upset his wife, he selected the next quickest way to inflict the most pain. "You are angry I have known Surina's cunt and you have not."

Surina gasped, alerting Kritan that he'd wronged her with his words, not only Rawlin. That was not what he'd intended to do. Far from it.

His gaze swept to her. To apologize in front of the guard would be to show another weakness, and he'd shown too many before Rawlin already. He was a king. He bowed to no one.

Except perhaps his wife, who currently looked as if she were entertaining removing his cock with her bare hands. He winced. Enraging the woman who would sleep next to him the rest of his days was unwise. She and she alone would have access to his cock, and if she didn't go so far as to remove it, she might very well decide to deny him use of it.

She squared her shoulders, a haughty expression on her face as she walked and stood next to Rawlin. "Let us do what needs to be done."

Kritan cursed his foolish tongue and followed his mate and Rawlin into the tavern. At least his manhood was intact.

If you can call fearing your woman's wrath 'intact'.

The smell of rotting corpses assailed him once more and he shuddered, thinking of the Fornication Hags. As if on command they appeared in the seemingly empty tavern. It was too early for patrons. No longer were the hags naked and chained together through rings that rang along the ceiling. They were free-standing now. They wore sheer dresses, their long, white hair missing in some spots.

Surina eased closer to Rawlin, her arm looping through his, causing a twinge of possessiveness to shoot through Kritan. He greatly disliked seeing his mate cling to another man.

The hags glanced in his direction momentarily, but then went to their knees quickly, bowing their heads in unison, their arms outstretched to Rawlin. They touched his booted feet, rubbing at his legs.

"Master," they said, speaking as one. He had thought them unnerving before. Speaking in unison upped that tremendously. "State your wish."

Master?

Rawlin was who held their leash? The tavern was his doing? No. But as Kritan watched the man approach the hags, Surina still at his side, and touch each hag's head, he knew he was wrong. Rawlin was the magik behind the tavern.

Had he been behind Kritan's ambush as well? Had he lied?

Rawlin twisted slightly and locked gazes with Kritan. "No. I had no knowledge of your arrival here weeks ago, nor was I part of the plot to capture you. Had I known of it, I would have intervened. And they had nothing to do with it either, so do not attempt to lay blame at their feet."

Kritan tipped his head. How had Rawlin known what he'd been thinking? Was that a gift of the High Magik Legionnaire Knights of the First Order? Mind reading?

With a snort, Rawlin touched the cheek of one of the hag's. "Yes, my lovely, the beast race does have a narrow way of looking at something. He cannot understand that we speak with our minds. We are of the same land and time."

Lovely?

Kritan's stomach turned. Rawlin found the hags attractive? Was that why he was no longer in the lands of the Valley of the Dead? Was he considered defective?

"Master is not broken." The hag on the end licked her lips, looking at Kritan and then cackling. "Want your cock sucked?"

Surina jolted and held tighter to Rawlin, her gaze moving to Kritan. The hurt in her eyes and anger that had been radiating from her lessened greatly. All it took to win her hand back was a proposition from a hag. He would keep that in mind should he anger her again.

Which he had little doubt he would.

Rawlin laughed and touched his side. "Ladies, do not tease him. We have not the time for it. Rise. I require your services."

Kritan nearly retched where he stood. He held no desire to watch Rawlin fuck the hags. He'd already seen them enthralling enough men—he'd not watch it happen again. "Surina, come."

She released Rawlin and came straight to him, her pace quick, her eyes wide. "What are they?" she whispered. "I can feel power on them. Old power."

"We are from a time before time," one of them said as they rose to their feet, staying near Rawlin, moving as one rather than three. "As is Master."

"What?" Surina shook her head. "He is immortal and has seen many years, but he is not as old as you make him out to be."

The hags shared a look and then began to pet Rawlin. One ran her hand down his torso and cupped his covered cock. He made no move to stop them and did not seem surprised by their actions. The hag who held his cock smiled, showing off her rotted teeth. "Master has much magik."

"Much power," the other said.

The third giggled. "Much passion."

Surina backed up just enough from Kritan that she bumped the bar. There was a flicker and then the holographic advertisement he'd seen his first time in the tavern came on. The naked woman cupped her breasts again, licked her lips and looked seductively out at the nothingness. "Drink up."

Surina bolted backwards and gasped. Kritan caught her around the waist. She looked at the flickering, poor quality image of a woman and then at Kritan. "Is that what men desire?"

"Not if they have a bit of sense about them," he returned, bending and kissing the tip of her nose. "If they are wise, they desire you."

Rawlin cleared his throat. "Ladies, I require your assistance. The House of Argyros is in need of a protection spell. It must be powerful and must last at least one full month. Enough time for us to see Surina to safety, to get Kritan back to his people and to have aid arrive at the House of Argyros."

The women drew back, shaking their heads, talking amongst themselves. They seemed locked in debate for some time. Each minute that ticked by, Kritan grew more uneasy about being in the tavern again.

One looked shyly up at Rawlin. "It cannot be done, Master. Even we have not harnessed the power needed for such a thing."

Rawlin's jaw set. "Tell me how it can be done."

The hags regrouped and then stepped back, the one in the center smiling. She pointed a bent finger in Kritan's direction. "If the beast fucks us, we could possibly manage the energy required."

Surina clawed at Kritan's arm. "Say no."

She had nothing to fear. He would not allow his cock anywhere near the hags. "No."

Rawlin snorted, appearing greatly amused by the hags' antics. "I agree. No. You are toying with him, lovelies. You know that would not create the power required to shroud the House of Argyros with protective runes and energy." The guard rubbed the bridge of his nose, deep in thought. "If I were to open a channel to the three of you during sex, would that be enough?"

The hag on the end pointed to Surina. "If you were to fuck her, the half-magik, half-beast girl, possibly."

Kritan growled out a warning. None were to touch his woman.

The hag in the center raised her hand, her finger aimed at Kritan. "If you *both* were to fuck her, at the same time, then yes, we would have the sexual energy and power we require to place a spell of protection over the House of Argyros for one full month, possibly even to the rise of yet another moon. No harm would befall those within the dwelling in that time."

As Kritan felt Surina's grip loosening, he knew she was considering it. He nearly shouted at her to return to the wagon, but the petition in her green gaze moved him. He knew she wanted more than anything to see to it those left behind were safe. It was in his power to help with that. Did he have any right to deny her something such as this? He had participated in threesomes before. Mostly with two women

103

and himself, but some with two men and one woman. Never had the woman been his mate.

"The beast will not agree to allow me to touch his mate," Rawlin said nonchalantly. "We must seek another way."

"His mate?" Surina asked. "This was said before. What does it mean?"

The hags giggled and swayed back and forth, much like young girls would. The center one spoke, "You are his wife, girl. His to command."

"His to love," added the other.

The third grinned. "His to fuck."

Surina huffed. "I am not his…"

She whipped around, her gaze on his right arm and the markings that had appeared during their first sexual encounter. Her jaw dropped. The next thing Kritan knew, she slapped him across the face.

Hard.

He touched his cheek, shocked his little flower had that much fight in her. He watched as dawning came over her. She gasped and touched his hand. "I am sorry. I do not know what came over me."

"I do," he said. "You are angry with me for not telling you."

She nodded.

"Are you not angry you are my wife?" he asked. It was a question needing an answer, even though he was connected to her now, already knowing she could not resist what was destined to be between them, any more than he could.

She bit her lower lip and glanced at the floor before shaking her head. "No."

He hid his smile. It was not an *I love you,* but it would do. He had not spoken the words either. Did he feel them? She meant a great deal to him, but was it love?

She teared up. "Kritan, we could save those I care for. You, Rawlin and I. We could do it. We could protect them at least for a month. It would give them a fighting chance. Please."

He knew he could not deny her and that she had indeed wormed her way into his heart. He was not yet ready to speak the words but he felt them. And he knew he would do anything she asked of him, no matter the cost.

He looked to Rawlin. "What will we have to do?"

"You are agreeable to this?" he asked, seeming surprised.

"That will depend," Kritan stated clearly. "I do not want your seed in my mate. I will not have her birthing your child."

"She is not my true mate," Rawlin said, a distinct note of sorrow in his voice. "Therefore, I could not get her with child."

The hag in the center laughed. "He cannot do what has already been done."

Kritan stiffened as the hag's riddle unraveled in his mind. Surina seemed lost. Rawlin's gaze went to her stomach and then to the hags. "She has accepted his seed?"

The hags lifted their hands and Kritan's right arm burned, another mark appearing, speaking of what they had already told him—he was to be a father.

Surina gasped. "Have they hurt you?"

"We simply showed what was to be shown soon," the center one said. "The beast knows what it means. What say you, beast? Master's seed can do no harm. Yours has already been sown."

Kritan could not speak. He was to be a father? The gods, whom he'd stopped believing in long ago, had taken pity on him. They'd taken him on a path far from home, tempted him with the possibility of seeing his brother again, only to rip that way, but in return he had gained a wife and a child.

His wife looked to him now, desperation in her eyes.

"I will do what is needed to ensure her loved ones are safe and cared for. Let us begin. But know this, I will agree to this only once. After this, Magik, you are to never touch my woman again."

Chapter Ten

Nervous and feeling lost as to what to do, Surina allowed Kritan to usher her past the old women and down a darkened corridor. Peeling paint lined the walls and she couldn't help but think the oil lamps that hung from the ceiling were only for show, for they barely put off any light. Each step she took, her stomach knotted more.

Rawlin and the hags followed close behind. Rawlin's footsteps were soft, barely there for a man of his size, much like Kritan. She suspected it had something to do with the warrior in them both. The hags made no sound at all save their periodic cackles.

Kritan stiffened as they passed one of the rooms but kept moving her forward. She knew he did not want to be within the tavern. That he had apparently been ambushed there. Her heart broke for him. He was enduring this for her, for her people.

Her love of him grew.

"There," Rawlin said. "The last room on the right. It is large and will do."

Grunting, Kritan led Surina to the room he'd been instructed to. She could sense how much he disliked the idea of sharing her with Rawlin. She was torn. She wanted her friends and loved ones safe and would do anything for them and she had always held an attraction for Rawlin. But, as the hags had pointed out, Kritan was her husband now. Though he had not wed her as the Tamoni would—only as the beasts of the Katarian would. He held the lion's share of her heart even though she had yet to tell him as much.

She entered the back room and her gaze went instantly to the large bed there. Her hands seemed to have minds of their own as they moved about, fluttering from nerves. Could she do this? Could she have sex with two men at once? A gnawing at her gut made her take a step back, directly into Rawlin.

He caught her by the shoulders, steadying her. His lips moved to her ear. "You do not want me as I do you."

He wanted her?

With a start, she glanced over her shoulder, her lips suddenly close to his. "Rawlin?"

Kritan moved in front of her, his hand going to her waist. "My flower, you do not see what I have seen."

She stared between the men, wanting guidance. "See what?"

Kritan's expression was unreadable, as she suspected he wanted it to be. He was a guarded man, she'd picked up that much about him in the short time she'd known him. "Your Rawlin, he desires you. Greatly."

"No." She wrinkled her nose and laughed softly at the idea of the famed lover of women wanting anything to do with her. He had bedded nearly all the women within the House of Argyros and countless more she knew passed through its walls. "He has whomever he wants. The women of the house whisper of his prowess and his skills at coaxing them into his bed. He has only ever told me that sex is bad."

Kritan snorted. "Because he did not want you to end up as you have—another man's woman."

She twisted, facing Rawlin fully, looking for any sign Kritan was wrong. What she found surprised her—raw desire was there in his gaze as he looked upon her. He clasped the brooch of her *palla* and undid it slowly. Kritan's hands began to move over her back, to her shoulders where he worked the tension away. She began to relax, her body starting to come on board with the idea of being fucked by two men.

Rawlin untied her tunic and it fell open, her breasts spilling forth. He simply stared down at them in wonder, as if he'd never seen breasts before when she knew very well he had. He'd seen many.

Kritan jerked her against his powerful frame and growled. She knew his beast was nearing the surface and that he needed to be calmed. Reaching back, she ran her hands over his upper thighs. She hiked up his tunic and slipped her hand over his erection. He was long, thick and hard already. She stroked him as Rawlin began to play with her breasts. Any reservations she had about entering into a threesome ebbed away.

The hags remained in the hall. They began to chant, softly at first and then louder. She recognized what they said at least somewhat, having read about it in one of the scrolls she'd read from Rawlin's private stash. It was of old magiks, ones not used anymore because of the possible payments they required.

With the chant came the strangest feeling of power buzzing around Surina. She closed her eyes, her body igniting with want. Her nipples hardened and she stroked Kritan's cock harder and faster.

Rawlin's mouth covered hers and the power continued to pulse around her. Her tongue greeted Rawlin's and she moaned into his mouth. Kritan lifted her tunic and caressed her ass, using his free hand to take over stroking himself. He slapped her ass with the head of his cock several times before rubbing it against the cleft of her cheeks.

Rawlin broke their kiss and bent his head, his mouth going to her nipples. He licked each one, watching her the entire time as if to gauge her reaction. She merely remained pliable between them, letting the alpha men near her lead the event.

Rawlin cupped and fondled her breasts, teasing them with his mouth as Kritan continued to sweetly tempt her ass with his cock. She ran her hands over Rawlin's chest, wanting his tunic gone so that she could feel him. Grinning, he undid his cloak first and then tossed his sword aside. He stepped back and pulled his tunic over his head and

109

stood before her in all his naked glory. While toned in every sense of the word, he lacked a lot of Kritan's bulk. She wondered it if had to do with the fact Kritan was a beast shifter.

Rawlin touched his cock and stroked it, his gaze going to her breasts. Kritan picked that moment to undo the cord around her waist, causing her tunic to fall to the floor in a puddle at her feet. She stepped out of it and kicked it aside. Standing naked before both men, she felt wanton and free. As if she'd been created to tempt men of power and strength.

The buzz of power swarmed around her, increasing her desire. She wanted to be fucked and soon. She turned, knowing who would give her what she wanted first.

Kritan.

He tossed his tunic to the side and stared hungrily at her before lifting her in his arms. She wrapped her legs around his waist and he speared her pussy, driving deep, giving her what she craved. Crying out, she held to him while tossing her head back, riding him as best she could.

Rawlin eased up behind her and stroked her shoulders first, then her back. He ran a hand down to her ass and shocked her by inserting a finger into her anus. Her body tightened on it as well as Kritan's cock. Rawlin chuckled and bit lightly at her shoulder.

Kritan pulled her off his cock and she cried out, wanting on it again, wanting the pleasure she knew it could bring her. He grinned, manly pride upon his face as he led her to the bed, eased her onto it on her hands and knees, turned her around and pushed on her shoulders, forcing her to bend. She did. He moved onto the bed as well and drove his cock into her pussy hard and deep.

Rawlin made his way onto the bed right before her, his cock bobbing in her face. She stared at it a moment and then did what felt right—she licked it. He guided it into her mouth and she relaxed, letting him do what he wanted.

She was so full. A cock in her pussy. A cock in her mouth.

Rawlin's cock nearly made her choke. It took her a moment to realize she had to fully relax and not fight it. As soon as she did, he increased his thrusts and made strange noises that she hoped meant he was enjoying it.

She was.

Kritan pounded into her from behind, his cock dragging against a sensitive spot deep inside her, taking her so close to coming she wasn't sure why she hadn't.

She clawed at the covers on the bed, needing release but being denied it. Kritan reached around and tweaked her clit, driving her even further over the edge of sanity. She sucked harder on Rawlin's cock, adding her teeth lightly. He pulled free from her mouth and bent, stroking his cock as he found her lips with his own. He tongued her, kissing her to the point she was moaning.

"Surina, I know you wish for release. It cannot be until enough power has been collected. The hags will deny your orgasm, but grant Kritan and I many during this experience."

That hardly seemed fair to her.

Rawlin kissed her again. "When you do come, it will be so long and so hard you will more than likely pass out from it and sleep for hours. It is why they deny you this now. We all require you to be active in this."

Kritan slammed into her, his cock twitching, her pussy milking it, still teetering on the edge of bliss. She cried out and clawed at Rawlin's arms. Kritan pulled free from her, and the sound of his cock leaving her was loud and sounded wet.

"Already I am hard and want for more," he said over the growing sounds of the hags' chants. "Come, Magik. You may sample my woman's cunt."

Kritan and Rawlin changed places and Surina looked lovingly up at her husband before taking his cock into her mouth. It tasted of her. She smiled on it and sucked sweetly, drawing animal sounds from him.

Rawlin moved behind her and then eased into her pussy. He entered her inch by teasing inch before settling into her fully. Her low stomach tightened with need. It was as if her body craved seed and would not settle for what it had already been gifted. She understood then what the hags were doing and she wasn't sure she'd survive it. It felt too good.

She used a hand to help cover more of Kritan's cock as she sucked on him. He controlled his thrusts into her mouth. She was thankful for that.

Without warning, Rawlin slapped her ass cheek as he pummeled into her from behind. Pain raced through her lower half but was quickly replaced by pleasure. He rubbed the spot and did so again. He repeated the action on her other cheek and by the time he'd finished, she could feel the juices dripping from her wanting cunt.

Kritan roared and hot seed poured down her throat as his cock pulsed in her mouth. She swallowed down his offering, the buzz of power increasing even more. As it built, so did her hunger for more sex, for more pleasure. And she wanted to orgasm. Needed to. She'd burn up alive if she didn't. She was sure of it.

Rawlin pounded into her and held still, releasing himself in her. Power ignited around them, aglow and alive. She would have reached out to touch it but exhaustion won out. She swayed and fell forward on the bed. Rawlin slapped her ass playfully again.

Kritan lifted her and lay on the bed, drawing her up and over him. She sat astride him, so tired and so in need of an orgasm that she knew she'd hurt someone soon to get it.

He laughed. "Wild woman. I like this need in you."

She eased onto his hard cock, her pussy soaked from the aftermath of each man coming in her and her own excitement.

Kritan moved her hips, forcing her to ride him, and she was happy for that. She was exhausted and her body ached for a full release. One that was still denied to her.

Rawlin stepped away a moment and returned with a jar of something. He coated his fingers. He pushed a finger into her ass again and her body fought the intrusion. "Breathe, Surina," he said, his lips against her ear, his back pressed to hers. "Push down and you will accept me."

She did and the pain eased away. He added another finger and Kritan stopped pumping into her. He held still as Rawlin lined his cock up with her ass. She was about to protest. The idea of something as large as a cock in her ass scared her. Kritan pinched her nipple hard and rammed deep in her. Pleasure assaulted her, wave after wave of it, wringing through her body. She cried out as Rawlin entered her, filling her to the brink of breaking, yet managing to feel glorious all at the same time.

The men thrust in and out of her, finding a rhythm, keeping pace with one another as the power swirled around them all. The magik was thick enough to touch. Everything around her was intensified. Each man's grunts and growls of passion increased and fell into a rhythm that reminded her of ceremonial drums. Their thrusts timed with it all and the magik continued to fill the room. It slinked over her skin, magnifying her sexual awareness, making her body pulse with additional gratification.

Surina gasped and panted, unable to think upon anything more than the feeling of being filled by two men. Her toes began to tingle and the sensation moved up her legs, over her inner thighs before centering in her sex. Insurmountable pleasure tore free from her. She screamed out as she struck her zenith. The men found their finish as well, each staying locked inside her.

Brilliant colors burst free around them from the gathered power. Surina watched in wonder as the colors filtered through the room, swirling around her, easing over her body, bringing a smile to her face before it whisked out of the room, towards the hall and the hags.

"Beautiful," she managed, just barely.

Kritan laughed a manly laugh. "Yes. You are."

"The colors."

Rawlin kissed her shoulder. "Your beauty surpasses it."

The last thing she remembered was falling forward onto Kritan's chest, thinking they had gained the power needed to keep her loved ones safe.

Chapter Eleven

"Wake, my flower," Kritan whispered, pushing stray strands of Surina's dark hair from her face. He kissed her lips, his hand going to her breast. He traced a circle around her nipple as he watched her sleep. She'd been out since they'd finished their gathering of power for the hags. He knew she was exhausted. He couldn't blame her. His wife was not yet worldly to the ways of men and women, and already she'd known him and another.

He gritted his teeth, disliking the fact he'd had to share her with Rawlin. He eased from the bed, seeing that she would not yet stir, regardless how much he wished to be on their way. He left the room and neared a window. Dusk was upon them. Soon the tavern would fill with patrons and possibly more of the Tamonius army. Something they did not need.

He walked down the hall, unconcerned with his nakedness. All present had seen him naked and fucking. What did it matter now?

The hags were in the main room, gathered, their hands joined as they stood in a circle, tilting to and fro. Their dresses were open in the front now, letting any who passed see their breasts and cunts. He shuddered but continued on to where Rawlin stood, as naked as he.

"How goes it?" Kritan asked.

Rawlin nodded, surveying the hags' actions. "They are nearly done."

"The house will be protected?" He certainly hoped so or he'd shared his wife with another for no reason. He wanted to hate Rawlin, but there was something he found himself liking about the man.

"It will. At least for a month." Rawlin faced the doorway. "That will give us time to get to Katarian and for me to amass enough support for a rebellion here."

"You think I would not send troops?" he questioned, wondering why the man held such a low opinion of him. "My wife's people are in need. I will send help."

"Kritan, you are a young king."

"I am nearly two-hundred summers," he countered, arrogance in his voice.

"And I have seen far, far more summers than that," Rawlin confessed, putting a hand to the wall and bowing his head. "I have seen men with good intentions cause wars that span worlds. I have seen those bent on destruction only truly destroy themselves. Life is fickle and one does not always know what one is in store for or what one's journey holds."

"You are a knight from the Valley of the Dead?"

Rawlin kept his head bent and raised his shoulders. "Once. Yes. I am no one now. I have no lands. No title. No king."

"A king sits upon his throne in the Valley of the Dead." Kritan knew little of the residing king, only that he held his purchase on the lands close at hand and that he had closed the borders to the kingdom, letting no one in or out in over five hundred years.

Rawlin spun and shoved Kritan. "He is not my king! He has no rightful claim to the throne nor to the lands. He is a thief, a liar and a murderer."

Kritan sensed a story there but knew better than to dig deeper. He held his ground and knew Rawlin needed for the mood to lighten and quickly. "Has this hole in the ground a bathing spring?"

Rawlin snorted, his lips turning upwards. "It is not a hole in the ground. I bought her nearly one hundred years ago. At the time, this was

116

prime real estate and to this day manages to turn a hefty profit, despite what you may believe."

"Unfortunate you did not travel with an oracle rather than the Fornication Hags. The oracle could have pointed out the neighborhood was goin' to hell."

Laughing, Rawlin touched Kritan's shoulder. "Yes, I'm sure an oracle would have said as much. The hags are handy and loyal. They go where I require them and are quite happy to serve so long as their sexual needs are met."

"You chain them during operating hours?" he asked, surprised the guard would do such a thing.

"Pfft, no. They do so themselves. They believe it adds appeal to their act. Nearly all see them as young virginal maidens begging for cock and cum."

"Have any ever seen them for what they truly are and fucked them still?" Kritan asked, glancing at the women.

"Yes." Rawlin kept his hand on Kritan's shoulders. "Two high-powered senators who are also born magiks know full-well what they are and do not see their glamour. Both come regularly and spend an entire day holed up with the three of them, having at it."

Kritan's eyes widened.

Rawlin laughed. "I know. To each his own, King."

"Will these senators help in the fight against enemies of Argyros?" Kritan's cock shriveled at the idea of men purposely seeking out the hags.

"Yes. Though they are no friend to him. If they do not, I will simply have my lovelies invoke the power of the thrall. Then they will have no choice in the matter," Rawlin said, as if that sort of thing happened all the time. Kritan wondered how many times in the past Rawlin had used his hags to get what he wanted. He suspected quite a

117

lot from the way Rawlin seemed to be handling things. "Plus, the senators do not want me to publically disclose their fetishes."

"You call the hags lovely. Why?"

"You look at them and see death and decay. I look upon them and see home. Much of the Valley of the Dead differs from what you would consider normal. To me, having no one around with imperfections is strange." Rawlin seemed lost in reflection for a moment.

"Is that why you settled in Tamonius?" asked Kritan. "Did the kingdom offer the most in the way of imperfections for you?"

"Socially and morally, yes. Though, this kingdom once held unwanteds, but they banished them to my homeland."

Kritan looked at Rawlin, still naked and still unconcerned, up and down. "You seem like a far cry from imperfect."

"Are you coming on to me, King?" Rawlin asked, grinning.

Kritan lifted a brow.

Rawlin looked to the hags. "My lovelies, Kritan and I will be below in the spring. Continue your spell and see to it none enter the establishment. I will not risk anything happening to Surina."

"If someone dares to enter?" one of the hags asked, looking hopeful. The smell of the long dead seemed to increase and Kritan swayed, his sense of smell too heightened to spend so long in the company of the hags.

Rawlin lifted his head more. A certain level of defeatism emanated from him, as if he'd given up on much already. "Then you have my permission to do whatever is called for to ensure they leave."

"Even kill?" another hag asked. She looked at her sisters, her eyes covered in a milky-white film. She grinned, anticipation in her gaze.

Rawlin stood closer to Kritan. Neither seemed bothered by their state of undress. "To keep the queen of Katarius safe, yes, I will permit you to kill. But do not think to tempt my wrath or twist my words. We have played this game before, my lovelies, and it did not end well for you."

The hags couldn't have looked happier, even though they'd been scolded. Apparently, Rawlin did keep them on a leash of sorts—a do-not-kill one.

"Kritan," Surina asked, appearing in the hallway, a sheet wrapped around her. She looked tired still. "You both left the bed. I was worried."

"It is not a bed I am welcome in again," Rawlin warned, and walked past her as if doing his best to avoid looking upon her. "Come. We can bathe."

Surina's chin wobbled and Kritan knew she was emotional from the loss of her father, from the events that had unfolded for the spell and because of the child she carried within her.

My babe.

Pride welled in him. He had to squash it down. Now was not the time or place to gloat upon all he had gained, in spite of all he'd lost. Kritan went to Surina and dragged her against his chest. He kissed her. "He will come to terms with it all soon enough."

"With all of what?" she asked, panting in his arms.

"With the fact that you are my wife and that his time with you was limited to today. He has not found his mate yet so he does not hold belief in such a thing as what is between you and me. When he does, he will better understand." Kritan watched as his mate nodded, doing her best to hold back tears. He knew she disliked playing with Rawlin's emotions. His wife was pure of heart. "Surina, let us bathe. The warmth of the springs will help to ease the discomfort I am sure your body feels."

She blushed.

He took her hand in his. "I can still smell your cunt. It drives me mad."

She tensed.

He grunted. "I should not say such things. They are crass."

"No," she said, tugging on his hand. "I like when you say what you're thinking and I like when you are thinking about me."

He lifted her hand and kissed the back of it. "Then you should know that since I met you, you are all I think about."

She blushed more.

He eased closer to her, pushing her against the hallway wall. "For instance, now I am thinking about how good your pussy feels wrapped around my cock."

"Kritan."

He kissed her, shutting her up. He ran a hand down the length of her and pushed the sheet out of the way. He slid his fingers through her slit and to her tight cunt. He locked gazes with her. "And now I am thinking of fucking you against this wall, to remind you who it is you belong to."

"I know who I belong to," she said.

"Do you? Because I sense the pain you carry for Rawlin," he said. "I sense that you want to go to him and try to ease it and the only way to ease it is to fuck him."

She shook her head. "No. He is my friend. I would talk with him."

"He does not want your words, my flower. He wants your cunt." Kritan snorted.

She tried to pull away from him. "Then he is different from you how?"

Stung by her statement, Kritan eased back slightly. "You think my only want from you is sex?"

120

"Is it not?"

"Surina."

She pivoted and headed in the direction Rawlin had gone off in. Kritan hurried behind her and caught her arm, spinning her to face him. "Do not walk away from me in anger, Wife. When you are upset, tell me why and how to fix it. For I am male and I will most certainly make a mess of things if left to my own devices."

The hurt moved off her face and was replaced by an amused smile. "Yes. You would."

He winked. "See. Speaking to me can make it better."

"So could stomping on your foot. I held back on that one though." She went to her tiptoes and kissed him. "Now, I wish to soak in the springs. My body feels as if it were trampled upon by a marching army."

Kritan grinned.

Chapter Twelve

Unus did not appear to slumber. Surina had wanted to sleep through the night in a room at the tavern in Vesta, exhausted from their sexual encounter, but the men had warned that they had spent too long in Vesta as it was and the threat to her grew with each hour they delayed. Reluctantly, she'd agreed and they had only just reached Unus.

Since their arrival, the night had grown darker, yet the people walking about had increased, rather than decreased. She had thought Vesta filled to the brim with life and excitement. It paled compared to Unus. The *angiportus* they were currently upon was so narrow she had already bumped into more people than she could count despite the fact Rawlin and Kritan were doing their best to keep her between them. Taverns, shops, vendors and places of rest littered the street.

Unsavory-looking characters continued trying to get them to partake in this illegal activity or that. The number of women selling their bodies for nearly no coin was staggering. Surina had never seen such things and suddenly felt so very sheltered. Her father had been right to keep this side of Tamonius from her. It was deplorable.

She took a long, slow breath, her thoughts going to her father. She laced her hand tighter in Kritan's as they walked, mournful he would never get to meet her father—never know what a kind man he had been and what a fierce negotiator he'd been. Rawlin had talked of times long past when her father had fought in the wars. Since her father had not appeared more than thirty summers of age, regardless his true count, she had often tried to picture him in guard clothing, such as what Rawlin wore. She could not. To her he had always just been her father and was not a violent man.

And now he was gone.

Never to know her husband. Never again to hug her and tell her all would be just fine come morning light.

Moisture found its way to her eyes, flooding them and making it hard for her to see. That was for the best. The streets of Unus held nothing she wanted to witness. Yet another whore stepped forth from a stoop, her tunic tattered, her breasts hanging out and dirt smeared upon her face as if a bath was foreign to her. She shook her saggy breasts and laughed, sounding much like the hags from Vesta.

"Want some, boys? I can give better than that thing you're draggin' behind you," she said, pointing to Surina.

Surina narrowed her gaze upon the woman. "You smell as if you have given *it* to many."

Kritan faltered in his step as he looked back at her, an eyebrow raised. "Wife, you surprise me."

"Not me," Rawlin said with a grin. "I have known her all her life. She is full of piss and wind."

The whore snorted. "But has she been full of cock? Does she fulfill you both?"

Surina went ramrod stiff, her gaze going to the men as she thought about their time in Vesta. About having them both buried so deep within her that she had not known where she stopped and they began.

Rawlin flashed a winning smile. "Dear woman, she has been stuffed to the brim with our cocks and she rang every single drop of our seed from us."

"And then some," Kritan added, pulling Surina to him and kissing her boldly, his tongue dancing around her, making her body tingle with need. When he drew back, his gaze went to the whore. "And the minute I am able, I will have my cock in her again."

"It's like that, is it?" the whore questioned.

"Something like that, yes," Rawlin replied, hurrying them along their way.

Rawlin and Kritan kept her between them, keeping away those who were suspect in behavior. They walked the street, the stones relatively smooth under their feet. The number of people on the streets grew as the ports came into view.

Kritan twisted her and held her at arm's length. "I must find someone. You are to stay with Rawlin. I will return shortly."

Rawlin nodded. "We will wait in this tavern."

"Keep her close."

Surina touched Kritan's cheek. "Why can we not come with you?"

Rawlin snorted. "Because he knows those who can grant safe passage to Katarius will not do so for two magiks. But once they have agreed to his price, they will have to take us."

Kritan inclined his head. "Remain close to him."

"I will."

She watched as her husband disappeared into the crowd. Rawlin looped an arm around her waist and steered her into a nearby tavern. The smell of the place hit her instantly, making her sick to her stomach. She touched her nose and mouth, trying to stave off some of the stench. It didn't work.

Rawlin went to the bar and returned to her with a large mug of something that smelled horrible. She shook her head. He laughed and sipped it before pulling it away from his lips and staring at her in a strange manner.

The more he looked at her, the more she knew what he was thinking about. Having sex with her. Her ass felt full at the memory of their encounter. He'd spanked her in a way that had excited her. She lowered her gaze and looked at the floor, embarrassed by her wanton needs and behavior.

"You cannot even look upon me now?" he asked.

She closed her eyes and leaned towards him. She needed to feel close to him, to know that all would be well with time and that their friendship was not ruined or beyond repair. "The things we did."

"Are natural."

"But you told me the things upon the scroll were things no one did. Ever," she reminded.

Rawlin laughed but it sounded forced. "I lied."

He pulled her into his embrace. As his lips touched her forehead she thought about what it had felt like having him inside her. She'd always assumed he'd be the man for her—the man she'd end up married to. Until Kritan, he had been the most logical choice as husband for her. So much had changed in just a few short days.

She sank against his embrace and sighed as he rubbed her lower back. It had been aching from all the walking. Most of her was sore, though she couldn't understand why. She was hardly out of shape. Yes, the threesome had been taxing, but the spring water had eased some of it. She should have felt much more like herself now. She did not. She felt drained.

Rawlin set his mug aside and put both arms around her. He rubbed her back more. "Your body begins to change. It is only half-Katarian, so the birth will not be as anyone would expect."

"The birth?" What was he talking about? What birth?

He snorted. "Think upon what the hags said, Surina. About my seed being unable to take root in you."

She did as told and then gasped, her hand going to her lower stomach. The hags had said Rawlin's seed could not do what had already been done. Kritan's had found the mark? "So soon?"

"It only takes once," he said, something off in his voice.

She pressed her other hand to his chest. "A child grows within me?"

"Kritan's child, yes," he said, sadness in his voice. She could almost feel the ache inside of him. He wanted a family. She had always gotten that much off him in their many years as friends, even if he'd never said the words outright. "I am aware of this yet I am still drawn to you. I've had a taste of you now and I wish for more."

With a sigh, she eased closer to him. "That cannot be. Kritan said once and only once."

"I know what he said, but if you demand it, he would give in to you," he returned, his hands roaming over her ass. He cupped her backside in a suggestive manner. "You could have us both."

As tempting as that was, it felt wrong. She moved her hands to his cheeks and went to her tiptoes, her lips going to his. Her kiss was meant to be chaste but Rawlin took it further, turning it into a reminder of what he was capable of doing—bringing great pleasure to her. She had to tear her mouth from his or risk being weak and begging to be fucked by him. "Rawlin, I have deep love of you, but I am not *in love* with you. I am wed to Kritan, even though he has not done so by the way of our people. And I carry his child within me."

"But do you love him?" he inquired. It was a reasonable question. One she did not readily have an answer for.

She paused, thinking harder on it. She was about to say no, that she had not known him long enough to form a bond of love, when tightness swept through her chest. She saw his face in her mind and the idea of him not being there, of something happening to him and her life being devoid of him, nearly took her to her knees. He had not only brought her great pleasure in his days with her, he'd managed to make her feel whole, as if a part of herself had returned. A part she had not been aware was missing. "Yes. I love him."

"But he keeps things from you, Surina."

Sadness eased over her. "I know."

"Can you trust a man who withholds truths from you?"

She caressed his chest as she spoke, "I sense that he holds back much from me, but that does not change the fact I love him and I am his wife."

"According to the Katarian ways, only. Not by our laws," Rawlin protested. "By our laws, I am your husband. I have the paper proving so."

She stilled. "What?"

A tic started in his jaw and he swatted her backside before removing his hands from it. He ran a hand through his hair, stress radiating from him. "Your father drew up a paper stating we are wed. I was to present it to the senate should anything happen to him."

Her father had done such a thing? But why?

"Rawlin?"

He exhaled slowly. "I have the paper with me. Though Kritan swears he will never harm you, he has not been truthful with you as to who he is. Should he harm you, even emotionally, I will take you from him and announce you as my wife to the senate. His bond means nothing to them. He is not of our people."

"I am part of what he is, despite you liking to forget so," she pressed, staying close to him. "And I will not betray him. He will tell me all he wishes to tell me when the time is right. Deep down, I trust in him. As I hope he trusts in me."

"He stands in the shadows, listening to us speak," Rawlin said. "My guess is his trust is weak. He no doubt feared you would take me up on my offer."

127

Gasping, she turned to find Kritan there, staring daggers through Rawlin. She went to her husband and slid her arms around his waist. He tilted her chin and locked gazes with her. "I will tell you what you wish to know but not here. Not in this tavern. On the ship."

"Am I with child?" she asked.

He glared harder at Rawlin before jerking and staring down at her. "Yes," he said gruffly.

She stiffened. She had not expected a child so soon in their relationship or really at all, and understood how naïve her approach to sex had been. She and Kritan had not spoken of forever or of a family. He could hate children for all she knew. She was not overly experienced when it came to them and had never given having one much thought. As the idea settled over her, she realized she was happy to be with child, but heart-torn that her husband did not share in her joy of the news. "I'm sorry."

His expression changed. He touched her lips. "Shh, my flower. I am not angered by this development. Quite the opposite. I did not explain it to you fully because I did not want to cause you further stress. All that has happened is enough, I did not wish to put you or the babe at risk. Know that I want this for us."

She kissed his fingertips.

He bent and kissed her lips and then pulled back, glaring at Rawlin. "I should kill you, Magik."

"Yes, you probably should." Rawlin shrugged. "But you won't. Despite your jealousy of me, you do like me. Though you will never admit it to anyone, let alone yourself. Now, shall we be on our way?"

Kritan's hand found hers and she hid her smile as he led her from the tavern. Rawlin touched her hip, reminding her he was close. She nudged Kritan. "What type of ship will we be on? One that carries cargo?"

He smiled as he shook his head. "We will board an *aeris*-class ship."

Her eyes widened. "A flying one?"

"Have you not been upon one before?" he asked.

Rawlin glanced back at them. "Surina has not been on any ship— land, sea or air."

Her stomach clenched. "Is it safe?"

Kritan laughed. "Yes, my flower. It is safe. And much, much faster than by sea. We shall fly over the Iced Seas, our sails hoisted high, our oars rowing clouds. And we shall be in Katarius within two hours rather than two days."

"But I thought all technologies were banned," she protested. "And magik is not reliable enough to power something the size of a ship for that period."

Rawlin snickered as he pushed through more people. Kritan kept Surina close and did the same. "Certain technologies were permitted. After all, the Iced Seas are not safe to travel upon most times of the year. The Ice Men who live just below the surface have great hate of landborns. Going up and over their sea is the best option and the fastest."

They pushed through way through the throng of people on the narrow street, the docks in view. Surina glanced to the left when movement caught her eye. She had only a moment to process what she was seeing before a scream tore free from her. There was a flash of steel and suddenly she was thrust backwards by Kritan. He and Rawlin whipped back their cloaks, drew their swords and blocked the blows coming at them from the attackers.

Men she'd seen once before.

They'd come under the guise of friendship many months ago, visiting the country estate and speaking with her father. Her stomach twisted, knowing they were part of the group who had betrayed him. She pressed herself against the wall, trying to stay out of the way, but the street did not give much in the way of space. So much happened so fast she found it hard to keep up.

Additional men joined the attack, all going at Kritan and Rawlin. One of the men fell after Rawlin ran him through. The fallen man's sword scattered to the ground. Surina bent and retrieved it, unsure exactly what she planned to do with it but wanting to help in some way.

Rawlin's magik pushed out and around her and she knew then he was using his energy to try to protect her. While extremely powerful, he had most certainly expended a great deal of power during their sexual encounter—more than likely weakening him in the art of magik for a bit.

Surina lifted the sword and turned at the same moment an attacker was rushing Rawlin from behind. There was pressure and her body rocked as she tried to withstand the weight of the man running himself through on the end of the sword she held. She screamed at the sight of what she'd done.

Kritan twisted fast, his eyes feral. "Surina?"

Blood from the dying man was on her hands. She released the sword and the man fell to the ground in a lifeless mass. It took her a moment to realize someone was shouting her name over and over again. She blinked several times. "Hmm?"

Kritan grabbed her to him. "Are you harmed?"

"What? No."

He exhaled, appearing shaken.

She looked around and noticed they were the only three still standing. Rawlin came to her and removed his cloak. He used it to wipe her face first and then her hands. Kritan pulled her into his warm embrace.

"My flower?" He kissed her cheek. "The man had to die."

"I know," she whispered, taking a minute to gather her wits about her. She'd never killed anything before, let alone a person. As she thought harder on the men being involved in some way with her father's death and that the men had come to kill them, her guilt began to lift.

She glanced at the number of bodies littered about the small street and then looked to Kritan and Rawlin. They were skilled warriors. Any who would have doubted before the attack could not do so now. The aftermath spoke for itself.

She held tight to her husband and then forced a partial smile to her face as she kissed his chest. "We should be on our way. Other guards will hear of this and come."

"She is right," Rawlin said.

"Come," Kritan added, taking her hand and leading her around each dead body. They made it to the docks rather quickly and Kritan navigated the crowd with ease, taking them to the far end of the docks. A man with long, dark hair was there, grinning, gold earrings in his ears and a strange ruffled shirt on. He waggled his brows. "You must be the wife."

She simply stared at him, trying hard to place his ancestry. His skin was sun-kissed, but looked as though it was such all year round. His eyes were as dark as Kritan's and rimmed with black lashes. He smiled, flashing white teeth before running a hand over his trews. "I am Captain Sagionari. You may call me Sage."

"A pleasure, Sage," she said, extending her hand and bowing slightly. She rose, her hand still in his. "But is your ship airworthy? I do not wish to plummet to my death on your watch."

Sage laughed and pulled her to him, doing a small dance with her before passing her back to Kritan. "She is a keeper, my lord."

My lord?

Why in the world would Sage call Kritan 'my lord'? She was about to ask when Kritan lifted her and held her high in the air, bringing her back to him, his mouth locking upon hers. He rushed her up the gangway to the large wooden ship and onto the deck. He set her upon her feet. "Kritan?"

He smiled, looking almost boyish. "We head for home."

It was difficult to smile and be happy when all she could think of was her home—right now under the protection of hags' magik and under the guard of Lectur and the remaining men. The halls of the house would never again know the same joy they once had—when her father had been alive.

She forced a smile to her face. "Yes, husband, home."

He looked to Sage. "Your quarters, Captain?"

"Yours for the journey," returned Sage with a sexy grin. "Try not to do anything I wouldn't do."

Kritan's laugh was deep. Surina found her mood lightening as she clung to him. He rushed her past Rawlin, who winked and then stood near Sage. Sage saluted and then cupped his groin. "Do not come out until she is good and tired, my lord!"

"Oh, I do not plan on it," Kritan responded, taking her directly into the captain's quarters.

Chapter Thirteen

Gasping, Surina held tighter to Kritan's shoulders as he kicked the door shut behind them. He stared down at her, excitement in his dark eyes. "Soon we will be home and I can show you off to everyone, Wife."

She put her head to his chest, thankful she had him. Already he'd proven he'd do anything for her. She couldn't ask for a better husband.

Kritan set her gently upon the bed and then glanced around the room. As his gaze rose, going to the ceiling, she followed it. Rings, hooks and chains were there. At first, Surina assumed Sage used them all to torture prisoners. As raw, animal lust shone on Kritan's face, she understood what they were used for and knew they were about to be used on her.

She twisted on the bed in an attempt to flee. She didn't really want away from him, but she did think some distance might be good considering he looked like he wanted to dine upon her.

Kritan caught her around the waist, his voice deepening. "To run from a beast is foolish."

Need slammed through her. She wiggled her backside against his erection. "Then you should punish me."

"Oh, I intend to," he said, carrying her to the chained area. He bent with her in his arms and grabbed a wrist cuff. He fastened it over one of her wrists with expert care. He then did the other. The chain holding her wrists together was of decent length. Kritan took it and lifted it, causing her arms to rise as well. He looped the chain through a hook on the ceiling, effectively holding her hands and arms up in the air, above her head.

The look in his eyes told her not to challenge him. Not now. He needed this. He needed to be in charge and she wanted him to dominate her. She breathed in a sharp breath as he let a claw emerge from his fingertip and then used it to slit open her tunic. She stood fully exposed to him and her nipples hardened at once.

She tugged at the bonds holding her wrists. "Kritan?"

"Now, we establish once and for all that you are mine," he said, a sexy grin upon his face. He retracted his claws. "No other man shall touch you again. Am I clear?"

She stared at him.

"Answer me." He cupped her chin.

"Yes."

He ran his hand down her neck to her right breast. "Say it. Say you are mine and no other man's."

She ached for more from him and had to focus just to answer his question.

His dark gaze hardened as he squeezed her nipple to just this side of pain. "Say it."

Shaking her head, she arched her back to him. She enjoyed this game of his too much to end it.

He skimmed his hand across her breast, moving to her other one, pinching that nipple as well. Cream flooded her pussy as pleasure raced through her body.

She squirmed against her restraints. "Kritan, please."

"Say who you belong to."

She bit her lip, refusing to reply.

He slid his hand lower, over her stomach and to her mound. His hot gaze burned into her as he dipped his head, his lips finding hers. The kiss was hot and demanding, not tender as she knew him capable of being. It turned her on, having him feral and in control.

He ripped his mouth from her. "Say it."

"I am yours," she said weakly, wanting him to fuck her.

He nodded and rubbed his finger over her clit, exciting her more. "Now, do you trust me?"

She met his gaze. "Yes."

"Yet you allowed Rawlin to begin to twist your thoughts in Vesta. Did you not?"

She shook her head, moving her pussy on his hand, wanting more. "No. Never. I trust you even though you hide things from me."

He thrust a finger into her, making her moan. He put his lips to hers but didn't kiss her. "I keep my station in life from you. Tell me, do you like fucking a slave? Do you enjoy being my master? Owner of my slave note?"

She stopped moving. "Do not speak of such things. You know they are not true. You know my feelings on one holding slaves."

He added a second finger to her pussy. "I am nothing more than a fuck toy to you. Someone to do to you what your scrolls showed."

She gasped. "No."

He fingered her faster, making her shake and pull at her bonds. "Stop. Please. Let me speak."

He rammed his fingers in deep but stopped moving them. "Speak."

She looked into his dark gaze. "I want to know you more—more than what your body likes. I want to know what your head and heart enjoy as well. You are not my slave or my captive. You are my husband."

The edges of his mouth twitched. "I am far more than that."

He kissed her, keeping his fingers in her cunt. When he pulled back, he grinned. "You are my wife and my captive…for now."

She flashed a wanting smile, rocking on his fingers. "I am."

He put his lips to her ear. "You are also my flower."

"Yes," she panted, riding his fingers more.

"And my queen," he added.

Interesting pet name to call her during sex. She turned her head to kiss him but he kept his mouth just out of reach, his thumb rubbing her clit as he pushed his fingers in and out of her.

"What say you to that?" he asked, stepping back, taking the pleasure with him. He undid his trews and freed his cock, stroking it, watching her. "What do you say to being my queen?"

"Yes," she breathed. "Please. More."

He laughed, his hand running up and down the length of his cock. "Eager?"

"Oh gods, yes. Please, Kritan."

"Answer me."

She had to think upon the question. "Yes. I'm your queen. Are you my king?"

He nodded. "Yours, among others."

She bit at her lower lip, her gaze on his cock. She wanted him in her.

Tossing his head back, he laughed, the sound rich and deep. "I am cursed with a wife who wants me for my cock, not my kingdom."

His kingdom?

She thought harder on all she knew of him and remembered their first meeting, remarking that he held the same name as the king of Katarius. A king she knew Jaelyn had been blood related to—though she had never known to what extent.

Her eyes widened. "You? You are King Kritan?"

A nod was his only response as he continued to stroke his cock.

She growled. "Release me. I wish to...*grr*, I know not but it will be bad. Very bad."

"Indeed," he said, nearing her. He pushed her legs apart and then lifted her, his body between her legs. He pushed his cock into her and laughed more as she struggled against the bonds on her wrists. He eased into her fully. "You have eternity to scold me, wife. For now, let me love you."

Surina froze.

His cock went balls deep in her as his mouth found hers. She wanted to hug him, to hold him to her but couldn't move her arms or hands. She settled for eating at his mouth as she wiggled on his cock. He took hold of her hips and moved her up and down on him. Her body screamed for release. Kritan fucked her like a crazed man and then pulled free, denying her an orgasm.

She whimpered.

He set her on her feet and pinched her nipples again. He moved around her and swatted her backside before rubbing the spot. He lifted her up and unhooked her chain from the hook but he did not free her wrists. Instead, he carried her to the bed and laid her on her stomach. He used one hand to hold her chained wrists above her head and the other to part her thighs. He rammed into her pussy with his cock, his full weight on her back. He pumped several times and jerked free, pressing the head of his cock to her ass.

She tensed.

"Let me in, my flower."

She remained tense. He playfully slapped her ass again and again, making her giggle and squirm on the bed. He ran his cock through the juices of her pussy and then placed it against her ass again, this time pushing and entering her. White-hot passion gripped her as he began to move. She panted and grunted, countering his thrusts into her ass.

She knew he fought for control with his beast because she could see fur starting to grow upon his forearm. She relaxed more for him, giving him what he needed from her, total submission.

He pounded into her, his hand easing around to her front. He rubbed her clit and she lost control of herself.

"Come!" he shouted.

She obeyed, her pussy starting to spasm. He pushed deep into her ass and held firm, releasing into her. He pulled free and turned her onto her back, his mouth finding hers instantly. He kissed her tenderly and with great passion.

"Surina," he said. "I love you."

She couldn't stop the wide smile from forming on her face. Not that she would have. "I love you too."

He ran his hand down her stomach. "Within the year we shall welcome a little one."

She sought his face for any hint of how he truly felt on the matter.

He bent and kissed her again. "I do hope it is a boy. Girls are so very prone to mischief. Case in point." He tapped her nose.

She smiled. The ship rocked to one side and then the other. She screamed, sure they were really going to plummet to their deaths in the dreaded flying contraption.

Kritan stayed over her. "My flower, all is well."

"Are we being attacked by the Ice Men?"

He chuckled. "No. They would not dare to attack Sage's ship. He has an understanding with them that few others do." No further details were provided on the matter and she sensed, at least where Sage was concerned, the conversation was closed.

"What made us rock back and forth like that?"

He kissed her cheek. "We approach land."

"Katarius?" she asked.

He nodded.

"Kritan, what will they think of you bringing home a wife who is half-Tamoni?"

He kissed her softly. "They will think what I think, that you are perfect. And if they do not, they will answer to me."

"Undo me," she said, lifting her bound wrists towards him.

He shook his head. "Not just yet. For now, I feast upon your cunt."

With that, he sank lower on her, his face going between her legs. Surina closed her eyes as pleasure washed over her. His tongue moved back and forth over her clit and she ground up against his face, the after-effects of her orgasm still sending tiny jolts of pleasure through her. She lay there, growing more and more relaxed with each lick he made. The man's tongue was gifted, as was the rest of him.

He moved his tongue to her opening and inserted it, sending even more pleasure through her. She squirmed on the bed, her bound wrists still above her head. Kritan rubbed her clit with his finger as he continued his sensual assault with his tongue upon her pussy.

Unable to take anymore, she cried out in ecstasy, panting, wanting desperately to sleep. Another orgasm struck and she shuddered with the force of it. Kritan chuckled into her pussy and then rose, his chin slicked from her juices. He kissed her, the taste of her on his lips and tongue.

"My flower, you need rest."

She wiggled her bound wrists. "I need to be free."

He frowned. "Surina, if I set you free, will you run from me? Will you leave me for your guard?"

He thought she'd walk away from him and run to Rawlin? The raw emotions on his face said he was serious. She sat up as much as she could. "Never, my king. Promise to never leave me."

He flashed a feral grin. "You've my word, my captive. Now, what sort of ransom can I demand for you?"

She snorted. "If you do not undo me, I will bruise from the chains."

His eyes widened and he quickly worked the bonds from her and cast them aside. They made a loud thumping sound as they struck the floor. He ignored it, focusing on her wrists. "I hurt you?"

She touched his scruffy cheek. "No."

He exhaled slowly. "Do not scare me so, Surina. You are precious. I want for nothing bad to ever happen to you. Already you hold many scars on the inside. I will not stand for you to bear them on the outside as well."

She leaned up and kissed his lips tenderly. He eased over her and then groaned, rolling off her. "Kritan?"

"Do not move. I must wash my cock and then, I wish to be in you again."

She laughed. "You never tire, do you?"

"Not when it comes to you," he said, hurrying to a washbasin near a mirror in the quarters.

Chapter Fourteen

Kritan held his woman's hand as he led her from the captain's quarters. He grinned, knowing he'd have hooks and bonds of some sort installed in their master bedchambers once they were home. He very much liked having his new bride at his mercy. He had only just finished with her and he already wanted more. He hoped the constant desire to be inside her waned at least a touch, or ruling his kingdom would prove difficult if every hour he had to stop to be within his wife.

He smiled wider. It could be done. After all, he was king. His advisors would simply have to come to grips with his sex breaks.

Sage was near the wheel, patting one of his men on the back. Rawlin was close to him. The guard cast a sideways glance at Kritan and Surina, and it was easy to see the longing on the man's face. Kritan would make it his mission to help Rawlin find a worthy bedmate. The harem within the castle walls was of no use to him now. He would task the women within it with pleasuring Rawlin. Even if Kritan had the urge to fuck another, which he did not, he couldn't. Mating came with a lifetime commitment. He would never desire another sexually. Only Surina.

As it should be between a man and his mate.

Perhaps Kritan would be able to find Rawlin's true mate. It was the only way he could be sure the man would not ever attempt to sway Surina to him. And Kritan would be getting hold of that paper Rawlin had spoken of and destroying it. She was his mate—his wife. Nothing would change that.

Surina sucked in a huge breath and tightened her grip on his hand. He followed her gaze and saw that it was on the ports of Katarius. The ports were part of the capital city of Ianus, the place Kritan and many of the Katarians called home. His castle, though, was not near the ports.

141

They would have to travel inland more. Many had questioned the reasoning for living close to the ports at all and having the capital city be near water. The Katarian did not fear attack. They were a fierce people, and if any wanted to try to conquer them, they were welcome to give it a go. The past told of several attempts that ended in the massacre of entire armies at the hands of the Katarians.

It felt good to breathe in Katarius's air once more. Ianus was large, like Unus in Tamonius, but it did not hold the same horrid smells as Unus. It could not. Too many of the residents were shifters or at least possessed shifter blood and traits. They could not just simply throw their slop pots out a window and onto the streets. They had to be creative and their engineers had to come up with ways to improve the quality and smell of life.

Surina leaned against him. "There is so much green here. To which city do we dock?"

"Ianus," he replied.

Her eyes widened. "The capital of Katarius?"

A nod was all he offered, amused with her shock.

"Kritan, it is…beautiful." She sank against him more and he turned her to face him. He held her close, rubbing her back. "We will raise our child here then?"

"Yes, unless you prefer he or she be raised in one of my country estates. I can rule from any and only want for you to be happy."

"I'm not even within the city yet and already it feels so different from Tamonius," she said, her voice weak.

"Surina, do not mistake Katarius as being crime-free and free from social issues that mark all kingdoms. We are not perfect. But we are markedly better, in my humble opinion, than some." He tilted her chin and kissed her lush lips. He turned her and pointed out and over the city of Ianus. "Welcome home, my flower."

Sage approached. "Your friend tells me you have never seen outside of Tamonius, and that within Tamonius you saw very little."

Surina nodded.

"Then tell me, my lady," Sage said, nearing her, "do you like what you look upon?"

"It is stunning," Surina said.

"I suppose so." Sage shrugged and Kritan knew the man well enough to know he no longer kept strong roots in either kingdom his ancestors hailed from. Sage preferred the open air and seas to land living. And had yet to find a mate, so he sowed his oats at every port he could. They'd known each other a long time, and while Kritan trusted Sage, he knew that Sage's heart was no longer Katarian. It belonged to the open air.

He could respect that.

"Thank you for passage," Kritan said to his friend.

Sage waggled his brows. "Ah, think nothing of it. I enjoy bragging rights as ship to the king."

Shaking his head, Kritan laughed and motioned to Rawlin. He came and Kritan eyed him closely. "Are you ready for this? Once you set foot upon our lands and are recognized, you may not be so welcome within Tamonius. They will view you as a traitor and already you will have much to overcome with those against Argyros."

"He will be welcome with us, Kritan," Surina said, a strength in her voice that spoke to the level in which she would fight to make it so.

Kritan pushed a smile to his face. "Of course, my queen. Let us be on our way then."

Sage laughed. "Oh, mighty one, I believe the cavalry has arrived."

The docks began to swarm with guards all dressed in blue cloaks, wearing brooches that said they were part of the royal guards. He recognized a few of them. They were young but dependable. They also appeared very relieved to see him. Kritan and Rawlin were first to the gangway. One of the guards sniffed the air and drew his sword. "Magik!"

All the men aimed their swords at Rawlin and Surina.

Growling, Kritan threw himself in front of them both, his eyes flashing ice blue. His claws emerged and he held his arms out, ready to die to protect Surina.

The guard closest to them looked to Kritan's right arm and his eyes widened. "The king is mated."

Another sniffed the air more, his free hand rising. He lowered his sword as he pointed to Surina. "To her."

All the men lowered their weapons quickly and bowed, going to one knee. They brought a fist to their chests. "Our apologies, my lord. We smelled magiks and wanted only to protect you. We were not aware you were mated to one."

Surina's hand found Kritan's arm, helping to calm his inner beast. He retracted his claws, but stayed in front of his mate. "My mate is half-Tamoni and half-Katarian. We will honor and respect that or we—" He raised a brow at the man who had started it all. "—will end up missing our heads. Am I clear?"

They nodded.

He exhaled. "This is your queen. Surina, these men mean well. And they will never again raise a sword to you or Rawlin. They will, however, raise their swords in your defense. Men, this is Rawlin. He is a trusted friend of myself and he is head guard to the queen. Any questions or issues?"

None of his men said a word.

Wise men indeed.

"Let us be on our way. I wish to show my wife her new home."

Chapter Fifteen

The wonder of all around her was nearly overwhelming. Since her arrival on the docks of Katarius, everything had moved so fast. It had all seemed like far too much. Thankfully Kritan was accustomed to it. The entire way to the castle they were surrounded by guards and villagers, all wanting to be near her—their new queen.

She'd not had time to see much of the castle beyond the back entrance—through the kitchen. Kritan had insisted no more undue stress be put upon her. He'd carried her as if she were a child through the kitchen and up a servants' flight of steps, down a long hall and to what she guessed must have been his room because of the sheer size and opulence of it.

She had barely time to remove her sandals when the door burst open and a short, pudgy woman entered, wearing a white bonnet upon her head. She took one look at Kritan, lifted the soup ladle she held, and charged him.

Kritan stood perfectly still. The woman wacked him a good one on the shoulder.

"Foolish boy, runnin' about without a bit of sense in his head," she said, her accent thick. Her red hair sprang out in different directions from under the bonnet. She hit him again with the ladle. "Been gone near a month now, with no word. We thought you dead, you fool!"

Kritan schooled his face and Surina watched as he touched the woman's shoulder in a loving manner. As one would a mother or grandmother. "Ethina, I missed you too. I am safe and well. I am home so there is no need to worry."

"Did they not feed you, boy?" she demanded.

145

Kritan turned her by her shoulders and nodded to Surina. "Look, Ethina. I brought home a wife."

Ethina smiled wide and began tucking her hair into her bonnet again. "Look at me, lookin' a mess when I meet the queen."

Surina hurried to him, putting out her hands and taking hold of the woman's. "No need for worry. You look lovely. And it is clear to see you love my husband and worried greatly for him."

She nodded. "Been lookin' after him and his siblings since they were just babes. Oh, sure, they had nannies, but they all came and went. I stayed."

"Ethina is the castle cook and never a finer one has there ever been," Kritan said over the woman's shoulder to Surina.

Ethina blushed and squared her shoulders, clearly proud of herself. "This one here," she said, patting Kritan's hand upon her shoulder. "He's normally good about following the rules. Should be, since he makes 'em. But he just vanished near a month ago."

"Kritan," Surina said, in a scolding manner. "To leave without word? They must have been so worried about you."

He blinked and stared between the women. "Do not tell me you will both stand shoulder to shoulder when setting me in my place."

The women did just that. Surina put a hand upon her hip. "Husband, need I remind you that you were ambushed, nearly beaten to death, then sold as a gladiator slave? And from there, tortured and tormented more? Had they collared you with that silver collar you would have no head!"

Ethina gasped and then went at Kritan with the ladle again. "Got no sense, you. Nearly getting yourself killed!"

Surina had to pull Ethina back. She then stepped forth and slapped Kritan's arm herself. "Yes. Fool!"

Kritan laughed and grabbed her, dragging her to him and kissing her passionately. He slowed the kiss, his hand going to her low stomach. "We should have Ethina make you something to eat. The baby requires food."

"Baby?" Ethina asked. She cupped her mouth and then threw her arms out and hugged Surina and Kritan at one time. She stepped back. "So much to do. So much to plan for. It's been over twenty years since this castle has seen a baby. Deana was the last."

"For good reason," Kritan said with a sigh. He looked to Surina. "My only sister and youngest sibling can be quite a handful. She is willful and thinks I do not permit her enough freedoms. I have allowed her to go off and study abroad. Is that not freedom enough? She is but a child."

"She is twenty-three years and if I'm right—" Ethina looked Surina up and down. "—your wife's age."

Kritan paled.

The women laughed.

Ethina touched Surina's hand. "You are far too thin. Your father and Jaelyn warned me you were nothin' more than a stick, but I didn't believe 'em."

"My father?" Surina asked, confused as she stared at the plump older woman.

The cook nodded. "Of course. Argyros and Jaelyn both went on and on about you and how much I'd like you. They mentioned you were thin. I told them when you finally got here I'd be shovin' food down your throat. I can see I need to start straight away, especially in your condition."

Kritan caught hold of the frantic woman. "Ethina, slow yourself, woman. Speak clearly. Her father and Jaelyn could not have told you of her. They are dead."

Ethina lifted a brow and slapped Kritan with the ladle again. "King of the land and he doesn't even know his baby brother is in the castle or that his father-in-law is more than likely going to remove skin from his backside for darin' to touch his daughter."

Hope surged through Surina. She stared at Kritan.

He shook his head. "Wait. You are saying Jaelyn and Argyros are here, within the castle walls?"

"Boy, is your hearing bad too? Yes, that is what I'm saying. King, my arse."

Kritan lifted the old woman and kissed her cheek before setting her down and rushing to Surina. He swept her up in his arms. "You heard, right?"

"Can it be?"

"King or not, if you do not set my daughter down and allow her to come to me, I will remove your head with my bare hands," a deep, familiar voice said from the doorway.

Surina screeched and wiggled free from Kritan's arms. She landed ungracefully on her feet, and thankfully Kritan was there to right her or she'd have fallen. She ran for the man in the doorway, tears flowing as she opened her arms. "Father!"

He grabbed her and held her to him, bear-hugging her. He kissed her cheeks and teared up. "I worried something had happened to you."

"Me?" she asked. "We were told you were dead."

He sighed. "Jaelyn and I were the only two of our party to survive. When we heard tales were being spread of our death, we permitted them to go on. It was the only way we could weed out the traitors. We went straight to the country estate and learned what had happened there. Lucila wove a tale I did not believe at first. One of you running off with a gladiator and Rawlin. And in this tale she said the gladiator seemed possessive of you, as a husband would a wife."

"They are safe?"

Her father nodded. "There was a spell of protection over the estate. Nothing with intent to do them harm could cross its barrier. And we were able to call upon help from those we trust. Additional guards are there, in the event anything more comes to pass."

Relief washed over her and she had to fight tears. "Good."

"Surina, Jaelyn and I made our way here without haste. I wish to know more of this tale told to me by Lucila."

She kept hold of him, unable to believe he was really alive. She thought harder on all he'd said. "Jaelyn is here?"

A tall, muscular man moved past her father and bent, kissing her lips gently before standing tall. He puffed out his chest at the sight of Kritan. Surina moved from her father's arms and swatted Jaelyn's upper arm. "Oh no you don't. You will not posture at him. He mourned you. He thought you were dead."

Jaelyn pursed his lips and sighed. "Having you as my queen will not be easy. You have had me wrapped around your finger since birth. I suspect it will only worsen now that we are all home, together."

"Brother," Kritan said. He didn't move. "It is good to see you again. Though I suspect your hate of me has not lessened over the decades."

"Kritan, we let a woman who meant very little to either of us come between us. I understand that now. And I'm not the same man I was when I left."

Kritan eyed Surina's father. "No. You were slave to this one."

"No," Jaelyn returned. "Not the entire time. I was captured in Tamonius and yes, sold into slavery. My first owner was not good or kind. After an arena game he was beating me with a silver whip and Argyros happened upon us. He put an end to it and bought me from the man."

Kritan growled, glaring harder at Surina's father.

Jaelyn put a hand up. "He saw me nursed back to health. He and his wife. She was half our kind, brother. And she had a large heart. I fought in arena games for Argyros because I forced him to permit me to do so. I wanted to pay him back for his kindness. A friendship formed. And I was there when Surina was born. Argyros granted me freedom when Surina was but minutes old."

Kritan's anger seemed to fade away. "Yet you stayed?"

"I felt very drawn to the little one," Jaelyn said, glancing at Surina. "As if I was meant to remain and protect her. And Argyros, Rawlin and myself work hard to attempt to right many of the wrongs inside Tamonius's borders. It is a hard fight but one we take head on."

Surina glanced away at the mention of Rawlin. Jaelyn noticed the action and took her hand in his. "Are you why Rawlin greeted us in the dining hall but refused to come up here with us?"

She nodded.

Her father raised a brow. The longer he stared at her the more his gaze narrowed. "I will kill him!"

Jaelyn caught her father's arm. "Ros, much was thought lost and many were thought dead. Was it not you who wrote out your wishes in the event you be struck down? Were those wishes not to see Rawlin wed to her?"

"Yes," her father said sternly. "But he is not wed to her. That one is!" He pointed to Kritan.

"That one will do right by her. You have my word," Jaelyn said with a laugh. "Plus, he has a considerable amount of political pull here."

"And he's father to your soon-to-be grandchild," Ethina added from her position near Kritan.

Surina's father gasped. "You are with child?"

She nodded.

Emotions washed over his face. "I am torn. I wish to hug you and kill your husband."

"Hug me first. Kill him later," she said, going to her father's arms.

Kritan neared and drew her to him. He extended his hand to her father. "Sir, had I been able, I would have asked for her hand from you, rather than simply taking it."

Her father laughed and took Kritan's extended hand. "Jaelyn explained mating to me. From what I understand you had little choice in the matter. Fate and your heart decided for you."

"That they did, but it was for the best. I tend to be a stubborn fool and I would not have wanted to miss out on a life with Surina. She is my flower and my heart. And soon she will be mother to my child."

"Do you love her?" her father asked.

"With every ounce of myself, sir."

Surina smiled.

"Then you have my blessing," her father said.

Surina laced her fingers through Kritan's, knowing that while they had won this battle, the war had only just begun. The road to peace between their kingdoms would be long and, she had no doubt, bloody. But she did know they'd be doing it together.

The End

About the Author

A pinch of fantasy, a dash of paranormal and a lot of erotic romance.

Reagan Hawk writes sexy alpha males and the women who make them bend with ease. To read more about Reagan's books, visit her website www.reaganhawk.com

The Raven Books' Complimentary Material

The following material is free of charge.
It will never affect the price of your book.

Strength in Numbers by Reagan Hawk

Born into a life of sexual servitude and trained to please men, Sempia believes her fate is sealed—her virginity auctioned off to the highest bidder then life as a sex slave. She never dreamed her childhood sweetheart would resurface in her hour of need…or that he would be the winning bidder.

Now a seasoned warrior, Eterin is nothing like the boy she remembers—he's all man and wants to possess her at all costs. But much has changed in the years they've been apart. Eterin has a new man in his life—one who wants to share them both. Sempia finds herself at the mercy of two incredibly hot and horny intergalactic outlaws who are dangerously close to stealing her heart.

Strength in Numbers Excerpt

The thunderous roars of the crowd shook the very ground she stood upon. So many had gathered to lay witness to the evening's festivities, celebration of the coming of the equinox, that it was nearly impossible to get an accurate head count. Varying moons surrounding the planet held their themed tributes for the festival. The moon she was on was for one purpose and one purpose only—sex. All Sempia was sure of was that she was the starring act on this night. It was she, a prized virgin from a line of sex slaves, who was to be auctioned off to the right bidder. Her hymen would be broken by the winning bidder and her slave note would then belong to him as well.

The entry of a sex slave onto the market and the taking of her virginity was a show many sought to see. They took great pleasure in watching the slave being serviced by many before vaginal insertion occurred by the man who would be her keeper. Much time and effort went into the preparation of the event and additional sex slaves were used to add bodies to the mix, increasing the show's appeal. The extra slaves were ones who had reached a certain status among coliseum goers. In some odd way, they had become celebrities of sorts to many. She could only dream of achieving such a status.

Long ago, she'd dreamed of a different life. One where she led a household of her own, greeting her bonded mate when he came in from a long day of laboring. A life where she would be thought of as more than property, but instead loved by one man—a man she'd selected already. He'd hardly been a man when she'd dreamed the impossible. He'd been a boy, barely older than her at the time. He too had been low-born, his options limited. They had been born to a life of servitude. And Sempia had wisely schooled herself to focus only on the future available to her, not the one she'd first dreamed of.

She had vowed to make the best of this life forced upon her. It would take her many years of sexual serfdom in an arena setting to win over the crowds in such a way. The odds of the person who purchased her note allowing her to continue in such a venue were slim. Most sex slaves were purchased for personal use and to be used to service the needs of those close to the owner.

Already the act, which would culminate with the taking of her virginity, was underway. She wasn't involved in the beginning portions of it. The crowd-pleasing regulars were used to get the masses eager for more and on the edges of their seats. She had to admit, they did their duty well. From her vantage point, just off from the staging area, the crowd appeared very pleased. They seemed taken with one of the alien species brought in to spice things up. It was hard to blame them.

Sempia tried to look away but couldn't as the Mantovian alien stood before the women in the ring. He was unlike anything she'd ever seen before. He had a row of four cocks between his legs, lined up vertically. They seemed to have a life of their own. Each one moved in a different direction, like tentacles. There was no mistaking the mushroom-shaped head on each of them. The rest of the Mantovian's body was a pale shade of blue, most likely having something to do with the fact he originated from planet Mantovia, which was almost entirely covered in crystal-blue water.

She could barely make out the gills on the man's neck even though she was well aware his species possessed them. He resembled a humanoid and apparently had close enough DNA to get him into the event, as all attending had to be screened for compatibility. Still, she wasn't sure what he intended to do with four cocks.

Space Pirates' Bounty (Strength in Numbers Series) by Reagan Hawk

Scheduled to become head concubine for a sadistic master, Lucia longs to be taken from her life. Born a slave, she believes she will die without ever knowing passion or love. Resigned to a life of cruelty, she never dreamed to find herself sailing the stars and sandwiched between two alpha males, each willing to die to protect her and each willing to see to her every sexual desire.

Raider, a Robin Hood of the future and a legend among thieves and space pirates, has amassed a fortune for himself and his crew. Seeking something more daring, he poses as a guard for hire and takes a position within a nobleman's household with an elaborate plan to claim the man's riches for himself. He finds himself less concerned about money and more captivated by Lucia—a most alluring bounty. His lust for her is dangerous and could leave them both with a death sentence. He doesn't care. He wants her and he'll stop at nothing to have her, to possess her, even if it means stealing her instead of gold.

Warning: Short story contains MMF/MFM (oh, who are we kidding, just about everything and everyone joins in the fun) graphic language, ménage and more, kinky alien sex, extreme alpha males, and pretty much anything else you can think to toss in for sexy fun.

Trading Teon (The Beast Masters Series) by Reagan Hawk

Garon and Lorne, shapeshifting males of the Ralenium race, are fierce guns for hire in the universe. When a cargo ship transporting women charged with crimes by the Galactic Star Union arrives on their planet, the men make the traders an offer they can't refuse. Planet Ralen is sorely lacking in women, and the males have an inborn desire to dominate, to tame females and to reproduce. When their inner beasts' clocks start ticking and the burning need to spread their seed consumes them, they go on the hunt for the perfect female. Too bad both men want the same woman.

Teon, a lady with a place in high society, thought life as she knew it was over when she was wrongfully charged with a crime by her stepmother. A prisoner en route to a barren planet to serve her sentence, she's presented with an opportunity to start over again on the planet Ralen. The catch is she has to be willing to be claimed by two males.

Not just any males mind you, two burning hunks who are ready to fight to the death if need be to share her bed.

Trading Teon Excerpt

The ship thundered and then sputtered to a stop as it landed. Teon pushed at the rusted walls of her cell, frantically looking around, wondering when the slave traders would come for her. She was no fool. She knew what they were. They weren't true Galactic Guards. They may have the badge and weapons, but under it all they were slave traders, pure and simple. Her hands, long since bruised and cut from the conditions of her cell, bled more as they scraped over the rough walls. She whimpered, the bite of pain a harsh reminder of her living conditions.

At least she was clean finally and out of the rags they'd been keeping her in. The traders had forced all the women into one large bathing chamber where they set about decontaminating them.

Her lips curled.

They wanted their goods clean and presentable. She'd been wrongfully accused of a crime, whisked away on a ship to be sent to a correctional facility in the far reaches of space, and then, before she reached her destination, her holders made a stop, selling her and so many of the other woman to the slave traders for nearly nothing.

Teon lowered her gaze. She could cry. The tears were there, ready and willing to fall but they'd do nothing. She knew. She'd shed enough already to no avail. The clothing she was in barely qualified, and by her people's standards she was nearly naked. She was a lady. Not some street walker. Even the harlots who worked in the pleasing dens on her world dressed in more material than the slave traders had her in. The material was sheer, allowing others to see her nipples and her sex.

157

They'd shaved the hair from her pussy, leaving only a strip of it down the center. They'd cleaned the hair from her legs and armpits as well.

One of the traders appeared. His head, very fish-like, was totally lacking in hair. They always wore masks of sorts unless they had tiny metal clips over the tiny holes where a nose should be. His eyes were slits and often his cheeks puffed out, reminding her of puffer fishes of old from Earth. He and the others like him sickened her. It wasn't their appearance. She was used to non-humanoids. It was their mentality that revolted her. The fact they made a living in the most deplorable way—by slave trading.

"Come," he said, the word drawn out in something of a hiss as he waved an electric prod at her. She'd been poked with it and shocked more times than she could count. As far as they were concerned, she had a bad attitude and she knew they'd be looking to unload her cheaply. That worried her. She wasn't a prize in their eyes, and that meant she very well could end up in the hands of even worse universe trolls.

She followed him as he led her down the long, dark corridor. She spotted several other female prisoners and their gazes met. The women looked terrified. She was too, but only to a point. Life on the prison planets was no life at all. She'd heard the horror stories. She'd seen the transmission sent out when the prison planets culled their populations—often allowing races who fed upon humanoids to come and "enjoy the buffet". Even being sold into the sex-slave industry was an end more desirable than a prison planet. Everyone knew that.

She shuddered.

The trader shoved Teon out the exit-bay door and she stumbled. He caught her by the upper arm, his grip iron-clad, sending pain radiating through her. She knew better than to whimper or show any more signs of weakness. They'd exploit it.

Critical Intelligence (Immoral Ops Series)
by Mandy M. Roth

Paranormal Shifter Military Special Ops Romance

When loyalties are questioned and bonds forged, the I-Ops find themselves fighting a war to guard not only their secrets but their lives as well.

Missy Carter leads a rather boring, overworked life as a system analyst for the State Department or rather, that's what she lets everyone believe. No, in reality her life is anything but boring. As an agent with the Paranormal Security and Intelligence, she's seen and done it all. Intelligence is her specialty, assassination is her hobby. The only problem is that the things she spies on don't die easily. In fact, some of them were dead to begin with. She's learned to handle anything life can throw at her. That is until the biggest paramilitary pain her ass shows up again. Lucky for him, he's sexy.

Roi Majors, second in command of the I-Ops, is having a hard time believing that Intel can only get half the information needed to bring down an underground ring of vampires with big spending backers who are hell bent on creating a race of supernaturals with multiple strands of DNA in them. As the team searches for answers, Roi searches for sexual release. When he finds himself paired with the one woman in the world who seems immune to his self-proclaimed charms, he can't wait to see her to safety and then bid her good riddance. He never counted on falling in love with her. And he sure in the hell never counted on her claiming to be an agent with a branch of the government no human should know about.

Rating: Contains graphic violence, explicit sex, and strong language.

Critical Intelligence Excerpt

Roi's cock twitched and fought to be free of his jeans. It dug hard into the zipper, leaving him shifting uncomfortably. Having Missy this close to him was too much. He needed to find release soon or risk dying from erection overload. Though he'd never actually heard of that being fatal, there was always a first time for everything. He could hear it now, "Man reported dead after having an erection last several days straight. Cause: Hot exotic woman denial."

He'd damn near passed out when he'd spotted Missy in the bar. After showering, he decided that he needed to eat and had the strangest urge to stop by this particular bar while driving by. It was as if something was pulling him, tugging at his gut and he was powerless to stop it. Having been alive a long time and having seen enough odd occurrences to know better than to question his gut, he stopped. The minute he caught Missy's scent, he knew what the driving force that called to him was--her. Who would have guessed that the one woman who hated his guts would turn out to be his mate?

My mate? Why the hell did I refer to her as that? Slap me with a stupid stick, or would that be a ball and chain?

Missy shifted slightly, allowing him a glimpse down the front of her red tank top. God, she was perfect in every way. Her breasts weren't too big, but not too small and the fact that she was so damn tiny compared to him made him want to protect her all the more. If that wasn't enough, every time she looked up at him with her chestnut brown, slightly-almond shaped eyes, he pictured what she'd look like staring down at him while riding him. It was so easy to imagine her silky long black hair falling down and over him as she worked that little body of hers on his until they were both sweaty and sated. If being sated was even possible around her. He'd never wanted to caress a woman more in his life. He knew that one taste of her caramel skin wouldn't be enough--it'd never be enough.

His cell phone beeped, indicating that someone was two-waying him. Unclipping it from his waist, he pressed the button. "Geoffroi here." He used his full name in hopes that whichever I-Op was trying to reach him would understand that he wasn't in a secure location.

"Geoffroi?" Missy mused.

"Where the hell are you? And, what the hell are you listening to?" Lukian asked sounding incredibly annoyed.

"Just getting a bite to eat, Captain, and enjoying the sounds of Styx … umm … just like everyone does. I just can't get enough of them. Did you need me?" Being submissive and cordial would no doubt tip Lukian off that he wasn't alone. If that didn't work, claiming to like Styx would surely give it away.

"Finish fucking whatever bimbo you found to scratch that itch you had and get your ass back here! And for God's sake, burn that CD. New targets were identified. My half-unit wasn't the only one in danger." Using the term half-unit referred to one's wife, or mate. Peren, Lukian's mate, had been the target of several assassination attempts. If Peren wasn't the only target that the group that was assisting Parker had, then more people were in danger.

"Make sure he knows that I'm not a bimbo and we aren't fucking! And tell him that I am not scratching any itch of yours," Missy shot back, huffing slightly. "As if I'd ever stoop that low. I prefer masturbation to you. I know where I've been."

161

Roi jerked upright, needing to adjust his cock soon or risk permanent damage. Running his tongue over his lower lip, he looked at Missy. "Can I watch?"

"Can you watch what?" Lukian asked. Roi ignored him.

Missy glared at him. "Go to hell, *Geoffroi*."

Roi stiffened, wondering if his attempts at wooing Ms. Carter could possibly flop more. Shaking the thoughts from his head, he concentrated on what Lukian was telling him. Peren wasn't the only target. "Roger that, Captain. Any indication on the identity of the targets?"

A slight buzzing touched Roi's mind and he knew that Lukian was attempting to communicate with him telepathically. It was one more bond that they shared. He focused on him and waited.

Roi, this is bad. I'm staring at a file full of photos and information on at least thirty other targets. We've also learned about at least two teams of ex-military men from around the world that have been assembled to 'reclaim' the original targets. And...

And, Roi pushed back at him. *It gets worse?*

The Barbarian Prince (Dragon Lords 1)
by Michelle M. Pillow
Futuristic Romance

Breaking up was never so hard...

Going undercover at Galaxy Brides as one of the prospective mates to these Viking-like barbarians, Morrigan has no intention of getting chosen to stay. But when Ualan of the Draig picks her to be his wife with the aid of his mystically glowing crystal, it is all she can do to say no.

Waking up from a drug-induced night of torturous and unfulfilling pleasures, Morrigan discovers her spaceship has left without her and Ualan is claiming she is his wife. It's not exactly the story this reporter had in mind. And to make matters worse, Ualan refuses to take no for an answer.

Being cursed by the Gods was never so frustrating...

Prince Ualan is like all others of his race on the male dominated planet of Qurilixen. He is raised to trust the mystic powers around him and when it comes time to marry, he is ready to follow those powers to choose his life mate. When the stubborn, yet achingly beautiful, Morrigan refuses to accept their shared fate and his supreme authority over her, it is all he can do not to break her lovely neck.

Rating: Contains graphic sexual content, adult language, and violence.

The Barbarian Prince Excerpt

Morrigan tensed waiting for the feel of a strap to her helpless skin. Her eyes closed beneath the blindfold. The whip snapped again and again. Each time she jumped, sure that it drew closer to her anticipating flesh.

Crack!

The loud snap came next to her arm, not touching her. She jumped, straining her arms against her binds.

Whoosh--crack!

It sung through the air to land behind her head. She jolted.

With each hit, her body grew more intense. The wood pressed into her backside--hard and unforgiving. Her body arched, dying from anticipation and fear. Then, gradually she felt a brush against her flesh. It wasn't the beating she had expected. Her mouth shot open in surprise. She could not see Ualan but she could feel the tickle of his whip as he dangled it over her flesh.

Achingly slow, it was dragged over a nipple. Morrigan whimpered, panted, cried out softly. The fight left her until she was completely under his spell. Nothing else matted but his will for her. She was tired of being in control, wanted to be free from decisions so she let him decide for her. Who wanted to think with the fog that was in her head? From beyond her touch-focused brain she thought to have heard him chuckle-- a dark sound, dominating and demanding.

The whip tapped and stroked her flesh. It brushed her thighs, kissed her feet. Then, as he drew it away another smack sounded. A gush of wind blew around her thighs as the whip crashed between them on the wood. Morrigan moaned, liking the vibration this action caused between her legs. She stiffened, too scared to move lest she get in the whip's way, but eager for him to do it again.

Very pleased with her response, Ualan hit again. Morrigan moaned louder. He watched her body strain and tense and his eyes turned a subtle shade of gold.

When she did not protest, Ualan's actions became bolder in his game. With a light slap, he hit the whip to her calf. It stung the flesh but did not hurt. Leisurely, he slapped her other leg, moving to hit upon her thighs. The whip's hard touch brought the blood to her flesh, making it tingle and burn with excitement. Next, the whip snapped her stomach. Morrigan arched her breasts, wanting them to be next. She was not disappointed. The whip snapped her nipples, both at the same time. Its stringy tip was like the slap of countless fingers.

"Yes," Morrigan groaned, past embarrassment, urging him onward.

The whip snapped her breasts again, this time more firmly.

"Ah, yes," she panted, no longer caring who heard her. Let the others hear her cries for once.

To find out more about these books or to read other books from The Raven Books visit www.TheRavenBooks.com

Rediscover the Magic of Reading
...e-books!

What you want, when you want it!

Rediscover the Magic of Reading!
Published by The Raven Books

WWW.THERAVENBOOKS.COM

www.RavenHappyHour.com